Charlotte Wood was named one of the *Sydney Morning Herald*'s Best Young Novelists in 2000. Her first novel, *Pieces of a Girl*, was shortlisted for the 2000 Dobbie Award and commended in the Victorian Premier's Literary Awards in the same year. *Pieces of a Girl* also won the Jim Hamilton Award for an unpublished manuscript. Charlotte lives in Sydney.

Praise for *Pieces of a Girl*:

'*Pieces of a Girl* is a compelling read, and although the material it deals with is sometimes disturbing, it is made easier for Wood's lyrical writing and her fascinatingly bizarre characters.'
Australian Bookseller & Publisher

'Atmospheric and stylish writing, compressed and highly focused.'
Debra Adelaide, *The Sydney Morning Herald*

'Lean and emotive, mysterious and yet immediate.'
Matt Condon, *The Sun-Herald*

'Immaculately polished style and lush, inventive imagery.'
Who Magazine

'There is something unmistakably edgy about *Pieces of a Girl*; a moody, atmospheric tension that manages to pervade this dreamscape of a book from the very opening page . . . A highly recommended debut.'
Australian Style

'Haunting, memorable, highly original.'
Adelaide Advertiser

THE
SUBMERGED
CATHEDRAL

Charlotte Wood

VINTAGE BOOKS
Australia

A Vintage Book
Published by Random House Australia Pty Ltd
Level 3, 100 Pacific Highway, North Sydney NSW 2060
www.randomhouse.com.au

First published by Vintage in 2004

Addresses for companies within the Random House Group can be found at
www.randomhouse.com.au/offices

National Library of Australia
Cataloguing-in-Publication Entry

Wood, Charlotte, 1965-.
The submerged cathedral.

ISBN 978 1 74051 264 0.

I. Title.
A823.3

Cover image of lily by John William Lewin, ca. 1790–1819, watercolour,
State Library of New South Wales
Typeset in JensonClassico by Midland Typesetters, Maryborough, Victoria
Printed and bound by Griffin Press

Random House Australia uses papers that are natural, renewable and recyclable products and made from wood grown in sustainable forests. The logging and manufacturing processes are expected to conform to the environmental regulations of the country of origin.

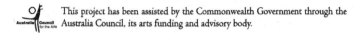 This project has been assisted by the Commonwealth Government through the Australia Council, its arts funding and advisory body.

For my parents, John and Felicia,
whose love story inspired this one

and for Sean,
with gratitude for ours

In my turn I showed him a postcard of my country . . .
He studied it carefully. At last he turned his currant-
coloured eyes to me and said,
'*Les arbres sont rouges?*' Are the trees red?

Helen Garner, *Postcards from Surfers*

Some private Eden shadows every garden.

Michael Pollan, *Second Nature*

ONE MORE WEEK and he is waiting, his heart faltering, on her front step. In his hands he holds a fish.

She smokes slowly in the bath, and the slight scent of it fills the house.

Later, she will tell him how impressively the bath-water holds sound, how in her underwater ears his door knock is suspended for a second, stilled time. This afternoon her half-closed eye has spiked the bathroom light globe into a yellow grevilleal star, and she is all watery conductor of the senses. So when the flyscreen judders and his knuckles strike the frosted glass, the sound of it moves through the fibres of glass and wood and plaster and iron bath claw and water, and it enters her body like a note struck on a bell.

Her hair is wet down her back when she finds him there on her doorstep with electricity rising in him, and holding out to her a fish.

Martin has been home for the weekend. He has caught the small bream with his line on the Pittwater beach in the early morning, pulled it flipping and sliding from the water. Has driven it, wrapped in newspaper in a poly-styrene icebox on the seat beside him, through the late morning city and then all through the afternoon, climbing the mountain roads to her door.

But now she is standing there and he knows he is only some stranger on her doorstep, yammering and gaping with the open mouth of the uncertain, the mad.

He holds out to her the newspaper and this shining platinum flower from the sea.

And all he knows is *Please take this fish from my hands.* His heart in spasm: please keep standing there, hand on doorframe and dripping hair and green dress casting its light on your skin, please open out your hands for this simple offered thing.

PART ONE

Martin & Jocelyn
1963

One

JOCELYN HOLDS OPEN her front door in the fading afternoon, water dripping on her neck, fabric sticking to her skin. It is the doctor.

She had first seen him in the grocer's, across the rows of potato and celery. As she strolled among the shelves and crates, shopping bag over her arm, she had idly pulled a couple of grapes from a bunch and popped them into her mouth.

Then she heard a little snort, and looked up to see a man watching her.

He raised an eyebrow in mock disapproval. 'I saw that,' he whispered, accusing. He wore a green jacket, was tall with pale wisps of hair. There was something about the way he stared at her, trying not to laugh.

She reddened, then leaned a little towards him. 'Your word against mine,' she whispered back. He chuckled quietly, from the other side of the wooden boxes, weighing potatoes in his hands. She laughed too and moved away. She saw him at the edge of her vision: an angular man in a canvas jacket, moving easily in a roomful of women.

Then at the counter he was behind her as the grocer weighed apples and pears and lifted her bunch of grapes onto the scale. She turned around. The man nodded at the grapes and opened his mouth to speak – but Jocelyn locked her eyes on his, and put an index finger to her lips.

He laughed again, and she left him there with his arms full of apples and potatoes and pumpkin in the dark shop, and she tried to stop herself smiling as she walked out into the bright street.

At a dinner in the town she saw him again, standing by a table and a chair with her blue jacket over its arm.

'Oh, hello,' he said, holding out his hand. His name was Martin, he was the new locum. He stood, slightly built and upright, smiling at her. As she stepped forward to shake his hand he said, 'Jocelyn, I have a confession to make.'

Her skin cooled at the way he spoke her name.

'I've stolen one of your cigarettes,' he said, and grinned again. 'I thought you wouldn't object to a little petty theft.'

Then he took her packet from the table, offered her a cigarette from it and lit a match. He cupped his hands around the flame and she hoped he could not see the slight tremor in her fingers as she held the cigarette to her lips, pushing her face into his bouquet of tiny fire.

And now he is here, standing on her red concrete step in the afternoon with something in his hands. He has slender arms and wears a blue shirt. Behind him the dark pine trees creak, and time slows and forms a circle. She sees this doctor standing before her as a school child with a satchel, as an adolescent boy with medical ideas, she sees him one day old and dying.

But here in this moment he is a young man offering her a fish on her own front doorstep. She holds out her hands for the newspaper flower. She is twenty-six, and she can feel the faintly shining fabric of her dress lying over her like a marine creature's skin. Her hair still wet, black.

She leads him through the house to the dark kitchen, and they stand there on the cool linoleum.

This is how Jocelyn comes to be cooking a fish in her kitchen for Martin, whom she barely knows. She stands in bare feet at the sink and scales the fish, and the translucent tiny skins attach themselves to her fingers, wrist, the backs of her hands as she grasps its tail. And Martin sits and listens to her talk, and feels his heart slowing in his chest. Watching her moving there in the early evening light through the window, until she is sequinned with it, turning and blinking, her moving hands braceleted with the silver skins of his gift.

Much later, his wrist trails over her hip and they smoke cigarettes while he tells her about the anatomy of the human hand – 'twenty-seven individual bones' – and relaxes his own long pale one to fall back hingewise from his wrist. He shows her how a hand at rest will always curl. He peels the skin for her, describes the moist red poetry of tendons, ligaments, their connections to the muscle and bone.

He has unfurled the skin of cadavers to see this. Drawn it back from the flesh like turning up a sleeve. And has been reverent, ever since, in every glance at his own hands; remains struck by a lasting (he thinks profound) awareness that it is the intricate construction of his own hands and finger bones which allowed him to witness the intricate construction of those finger bones, that palm, those elegant veins.

Now he holds her hand up and presses his against it, the larger one echoing hers, finger to finger, palm to palm.

Of all his boyhood, he says, he can recall mostly his hands: tucked beneath his head in sleep, or curved around a railing, a pencil, ball, shoelace. Then the realisation, at five, of his fingers' particular dexterity, and that understanding falling like a stone into water, and the lip of possibility forming in slow motion, pluming outwards. The radiating certainty of a future brought into being by his hands.

At five he had lifted a quivering pigeon from where it lay scouring a circle beneath his father's car with its wrongly bent wing. Reminding him of a stepped-on cardboard box. He held its jittering body away from his own, terrified of its smell and its plasticky beak. Then held it closer and pulled the bent wing gently outwards. The bird now only stared, perfectly still, the feathers oily between his finger and thumb.

And then a tiny jolt, and then – this is the moment, over and over again, the moment he cannot ever fall away from, like the first leaping flame in the memory of an arsonist – he felt the weight of the thing shift in his hands and then the creature shot up, arced, righted itself and flew a clear straight break into the suburban air. The last thing the child Martin saw was that wing spanned out above the street, and in his mind now he sees every bladed feather of that silver oar, dipping and rowing the rippling air.

He knows it is ridiculous, knows it to be a matter of an animal's shock and recovery, or a mild dislocation righted. But each time he's remembered it over the years, his five-year-old's shock and reverence returns. He is planted beneath a white sky on a suburban driveway, in his school jumper, his feet inside his grey socks and his shoes. Holding his hands out before him, fingers stretched, these instruments of the supernatural.

Two

THE LATEST PARCEL of galley pages is opened, and they cover the dining-room table. She sorts the pages daily, but they shuffle and spill from their piles. Almost halfway through her contract and she's up to volume six of this job, *The Complete Illustrated Encyclopaedia of Australia*.

Her proofreader's marks are looking tired, but even after all these months she's still drawn to it, to this sense of the continent spilling out over her dining room. Of the Simpson Desert between the dictionary and the telephone, opal mines under the coffee cup.

In the weeks since Martin arrived at her door there has been a sense of dormant things coming alive. One day in the garden, they crouched over a bucket.

'Did you grow that?' Martin asked, peering into the

bucket in which the white star of a water lily was prising itself open.

'It grew itself,' she said. 'I just threw a lump of wood into the water.'

'Then it's a gift,' he said, smiling.

Now, at the table, she reads, *The banksia germinates only after fire. It is one of the many tricks Australian plants must play to survive the harshness of the climate* – the years of waiting in the earth, and then after the fire has raged overhead and pieces of leaf-shaped ash still fall in distant towns, the pale fist unfurls there in the dark. And then a season passes, and then the banksia's red candles shout from the bush like another kind of flame.

At university Martin's classmates watched him examine a patient as though they were at the theatre. They watched him at the hospital bedside of a schoolgirl, his fingers pressed lightly at her neck behind her jaw, her eyes dark in her pale face, gaze steady on his while he touched her. They listened to his low voice, her whispered answers, and they raced their own thoughts with his.

But then he tucked the schoolgirl in, and smoothed her small hand before putting it gently beneath the sheet, and stood. As he walked away, when they heard him murmur – *meningitis* – it was instant, magic. What was invisible a second before they could now see clear as day. His professors had tried to talk him into surgery, or another speciality, telling him his talent would be wasted in general practice.

In bed one morning he says to her, 'When's your birthday?'

She lies back, arms above her head, knuckles against the cool wall. He has the sheet pulled to his chin, his large pale feet sticking out at the other end.

'August the first.'

For some reason it is the date racehorses' ages are changed. The horses' birthday.

His eyebrows rise, and he chortles, turning to her, lifting on his elbow. She can see a swatch of freckles on the pale inside of his upper arm. He leans in to kiss her, still laughing. 'Giddy-up,' he says.

When she was eighteen a boy the same age had asked her to dance. She had stood up from the folding wooden chair against the wall in her stiff yellow dress, feeling sick. The dress pinched at her waist and her armpits, and on her feet she wore white shoes with heels so high she had to hold fast to the boy's arm to keep herself from toppling.

He was a farm boy she had never met in this town, nor heard of. Who said the names of Sydney boarding schools as though they should be familiar to her, and who never let go her hand as they danced, and as long as they were touching she knew she could move without falling.

One night in the car the boy gave her a box with a ring inside it.

She did not know what to do, when you are eighteen and there is a ring. She took it from the box and held it in her fingers. He watched, and while she tried to find words she began to slide it onto a finger of her right hand there in the dark, their breath steaming in the cold. But he stopped her and took her other hand, and then it was both of them with the too-small ring, pushing it onto her finger, grazing her knuckle. She still had no words, but the ring glinted and shone like something definite. So she put her hand to the boy's face.

When she was with him people exclaimed at the ring, grabbing her hand and turning it to catch the light. When she was with him the light sparked off the blue stone like electricity.

But when she was alone the ring pinched and its sharp edges scratched and caught on things. She sometimes woke in the morning with a tiny thread of blood on her face. Sometimes she would twist it so the stone dug into her palm, leaving only the silver band showing.

Her sister, Ellen, made her turn it out again. 'You are so *lucky*,' she said, holding out her own small diamond, fingers splayed, for emphasis.

When Jocelyn was nineteen the boy would sometimes look her up and down before they went out. On hot summer days the ring tightened so she could no longer even twist it.

When she was nineteen and a half she watched him dancing with her friend, and saw the girl giggling with her chin tilted upwards, and she remembered what it was like, that warm hand on the small of her back, and she knew.

That night she stood in the green bathroom, scrubbing at the ring with soap under cool running water for half an hour. The silver dragged across her knuckle like a razorblade, and her joints cracked. When the ring finally tinkled into the basin her finger was rubbed raw, and where the ring had been her skin was narrow, white.

Afterwards Ellen and their mother would fold their arms at her and speak only in practicalities. Invitation printing wasted, a cake used for window display instead.

When Martin left university and went to work, he spread his pens and things about his first desk. The little surgery smelling of old books and antiseptic was an opening world, and he smoothed the corners of the posters on the wall, and dusted with his handkerchief the base of a creamy plastic model of the joints of the knee.

When he stepped into the waiting room to call his first patient, he had to calm his breath and stop his voice from catching.

And in these years, from practice to practice, from locum to locum, his instincts have never failed him. Curative, perhaps talented (he resists 'healing'), these safe hands of his. On the whole he suppresses any more mystical belief in their powers; in his mind he somehow transmutes magic into science. He has steady nerves, that is all. He is a well-trained, skilled practitioner. He listens carefully to what his patients say, and what they omit; he asks them particular questions. Is well read, keeps up with the literature, performs the proper examinations at the right times, has correctly practised their techniques.

So that when he touches his patients' skin . . . *other possibilities begin to form themselves.*

The first night they had slept together, Martin had said, staring at Jocelyn's body, 'I dreamed your skin would be like this.'

His certainty falls over her like rain. And when she is not with him Martin hovers at all times behind her concentration; she feels him like breath.

But there are times when she is alone in the night and the wind sounds like an ocean outside her window, and she lies in her bed, thinking, *What am I doing?*

The wind heaves and though she knows it is the sound of branches, in the dark she can picture nothing but black water swelling and contracting. An approaching wave that could drown her.

It is still cold here in the mountains, in the early spring. George is coming back to the surgery in a week and Martin must return to Sydney, to his house at the beach. The three months gone in a moment. One night when he is visiting her house he takes a breath to say something.

They are setting the fire together, kneeling among the bits of kindling and newspaper.

'That's path*etic*,' she says, pulling his crumpled bits of paper from the cold ash. She pushes up her sleeves, irons paper flat on the floor with her hand.

'I will show you,' she says, flourishing a page dramatically, 'how to fold the Standard British Firelighter.' He makes a face. His pulse jittering, waiting for the moment.

'I was in the Brownies, you know,' she says. He snorts, crosses his arms, and as she folds the paper he sees on it a photograph of a crumpled black-and-white wedding party, hats and flowers and patent leather shoes, a glum bride.

Then, triumphant, she holds up the origami shape for him – 'Now *that's* a firelighter a girl can be proud of' – and leans into the fireplace.

'I'm sure Brown Cow would be very pleased,' he says, covering up his waiting, making her chuckle as she pokes the paper under kindling.

He puts a hand to the bare skin at the base of her spine, watches her skin pricking under his fingers. She strikes a match, and he takes his breath.

'Let's get married.'

She sits up, and stares at him.

'What?'

He meets her eye, keeps going. 'I think we should get married. And you can come back with me to Pittwater.' Watching her face.

It is late September. Through the window her mother's garden is in raging flower. Azaleas, wisteria, forget-me-nots in balloons around the trunks of apple and peach trees. Irises, daffodils, rosemary. All winter the garden is washed out and grey, and then in spring it explodes into colour. By midsummer it is leached dry again, but all through the childhoods of Jocelyn and her sister their mother had loved this eight weeks of English bloom. Jocelyn now leaves it barely tended.

Her pulse is all through her body and Martin is waiting for her to speak. She stares into the fireplace, the damp paper smouldering. She holds her left hand in her right, fingering the knuckles. The skin of her hands is dry, her mouth is dry.

Martin cannot wait this out. 'What do you think?'

Jocelyn takes his hand in hers, stares out of the window again at her mother's flowers. She can't say, *There was a ring*. She can't say, *I couldn't get it off*.

'I can't get married,' she says quietly.

Oh, his beautiful face. He is staring at the floor, rubbing his lips, very gently, with two fingers.

'But I will come back with you. To live.' She says it fast.

He looks up at her now. It is 1963. They both know what she is offering: to hurl her reputation, and his with it, over the precipice of those sandstone cliffs below this mountain house.

He can't believe what she is saying. '*Why?*'

The azaleas waver at the window. She is ashamed, she picks at the hem of her skirt. There is silence. 'Because marriage is ordinary,' she whispers then.

She lifts her head, steady, and meets his gaze.

He takes her hand. 'But what about the neighbours?'

'I don't care what they think. If you don't.' Her voice small.

'What about your job?' He is stroking her hand as if to comfort her.

She sits back, crosses her legs in front of her, lights a cigarette. She is fighting the urge to cry. 'I'll make sure they don't know. It's miles from the city, isn't it? I can have the post redirected, tell people I'm spending a summer by the sea. People do that, don't they?'

A hand of flame leaps as the folded paper beneath the kindling catches. The wedding party shrinks and shrivels, the bride's veil aflame.

Jocelyn exhales, watches the smoke plume to the ceiling. She cannot say anything more. It is her turn to wait, and breathe, chewing the inside of her lip. *Please.*

Then Martin moves slowly on his knees towards her, pulls her close till she climbs onto his lap, and he wraps her around himself, his arms round her waist.

They are clung together on the edge of the cliff. They jump.

'Yes,' says Martin. 'Yes.'

Three

T HE WORLD'S LARGEST *and most famous coral formation is the Great Barrier Reef, off the coast of Queensland.* She holds her pencil above the line of words, over those underwater sunrises lining the continent's north-eastern coast.

Proofreading this part of the manuscript is easy during these first Pittwater days; here it is easy to remember that the whole country is bordered by blue ocean. She works in the shade of the verandah while Martin spends his days in the city.

It is early October, but the air is hot and bright.

Coming here that first day, when she stepped onto the ferry at Palm Beach, she crossed more than that strip of green-black water. Martin was already on board, holding out his hand to her, her luggage waiting on the boat's wooden deck behind him.

His neighbours, seated with their city shopping bags on their laps, turned their heads to watch the arrival of *the doctor's mistress*. She saw them watching, and her breath went shallow. And then she saw Martin's open, steady hand, and he beamed at her. She held out her own hand and put it into his, and he held it fast, and as she stepped across that gap she knew her childhood was finished.

He held her hand all the way across the water to the little jetty at his beach, and she tried not to feel her fingers quivering under his. She lifted her head to face a woman looking at her across the decking boards. Jocelyn forced herself to smile, and the woman looked away.

They were the first to alight, and the people watched them walk the length of the jetty, Jocelyn's suitcase between them, before they began to gather their own bags and make their way to their homes.

Jocelyn had to raise a hand to shade her eyes from the hard white light as they walked towards the line of new houses strung along the beach.

Martin had nodded – 'There' – at one of the newest. Its iron porch railing was wound with Neptune's necklace, the beaded seaweed he sometimes brings back to the house to garland the verandah with until it stiffens and shrivels, to be tossed over the rail into the garden in the morning when they sit out drinking coffee.

Jocelyn puts down her pencil and gets up from the table. Her back aches. She stretches, bends down to touch her toes. As her fingertips brush the floorboards she thinks of Martin on his way to work, his long drive through the bush and the beaches running alongside the road.

Since her arrival, the people from the older cottages, small buildings subdued by passionfruit vine and over-grown kikuyu, stare fixedly at the track as they walk past this verandah to swim, or fish. Occasionally one will grunt a greeting, but mostly they walk with heads down, shamed at these young people who will sit so exposed with their breakfast outside, at this bare house set almost amongst the waves, its doors and its windows always open to the gulls and the fish and the sea.

The mass of bush in the hills behind the houses meets the city's northwestern outskirts not so many miles away. But here there are no roads and they can travel only by boat or the public ferry from Palm Beach, making their small headland an island.

Each morning they wake with the sun blaring. They lie in bed, and Jocelyn listens to Martin waking up. She hears his breath change from slow to sharp as he first leaves sleep. She hears his yawn, feels the slump of his body become alert, his movement behind her as he stretches, arching his back. She lies, eyes closed, half-awake, half-waiting. And then, each time, his heavy hand comes to her shoulder, or hip, and he kisses her through the blankets while he thinks she is asleep, and then he rolls away and heaves himself upright.

Once she feels his hand resting on her, that moment's stillness, she falls easily back into sleep.

Whenever Martin leaves the house he is in the wash of this thing, this tide. On the drive to the city he thinks about past women, the times he thought he was in love; those imitated feelings, the flowers and the chocolates. No woman has imprinted herself on him like this.

He had offered her a gold ring that morning before they stepped onto the boat, to protect her from the locals' gawking. Before they reached the jetty he pulled the pawn-shop wedding ring from his pocket. She had held it a moment, and given it back to him.

'I do not need a ring on my finger,' she had said. 'I am not ashamed.'

But he could feel the gut depth of her fear, and when she stepped onto that boat, when she smiled into those staring faces, it was the work of a death-defyer, an acrobat.

He thinks of her working at the house now, head bent over the paper, chewing a pen. And then his car rounds the Bilgola bends and the sun blares over that curved sheet of ocean, and all the risk explodes like fireworks in the shimmering blue air.

Morning and night every closure of his eyes attracts her, their every opening challenges her. In the past Jocelyn has shaken her head at women like the one she has now become. Who would risk all their future, who were called harlots, who bore this shame in place of marriage. Their stupidity, their *masochism*, astonished her.

But she is worse; she has chosen this disgrace herself.

She straightens, goes to the bedroom to find her bathing suit.

She thinks of her mother, her father, glad they are not alive to hear the rumours she knows will already be flying about the mountains town. She has not told Ellen, safely married in London, about Martin yet. Again she remembers her sister's face, her mother's, at that broken engagement years ago, their disbelief. She heard them talking in the kitchen, and then Ellen cornered her in the laundry. 'You know there's something wrong with you, don't you?' Ellen had said it slowly, pity in her voice. Jocelyn could only finger the rounded concrete edge of the laundry trough. 'Yes,' she had murmured. She knew.

Even when her father held her hand briefly in the garden, and patted it, and said, 'Never mind', she knew that it was shameful, this want in her for more than she was offered.

But now, as she pulls the green swimsuit over her breasts and feels the flick of elastic on her skin, she has no shame, for she knows something else is happening to her. There is some opening up of possibility not to do with Martin, but because of him.

Sometimes, after three hours' work and only twelve pages of her proofing-marks, the frustration of this labour infuriates her, this plodding through someone else's laziness. She feels like a scullery maid, scrubbing the stains from someone else's clothes, picking up their mess. She flicks the pencil across the table, listens to it roll.

She walks through the house, down the front steps, across the lawn and the sandy track. Sometimes she suspects it is this early private summer, it is the sun and the water causing this planetary shift of her world. But she knows it is not the sun and the water.

She walks past the sidelong glance of the woman two doors down who stands watering her lawn in a chequered apron. The light is so bright she walks with half-closed eyes. Adjusting from the closely read print to the outdoor space and light, her eyes blur and reshape what they see.

The maps in the encyclopaedia have begun to make her see things aerially, turn the headlands into vegetation maps, the bays and points into geometric slabs and curves.

She bends to pick up a small turreted green shell and puts it in her pocket. Already she should go back to the house and the manuscript. She can almost recite the text waiting on the page.

Ayers Rock, the world's largest monolith, is six miles round, more than a mile and a half long and 1,100 feet high, rising from the flat surrounding earth.

But she strides over the white sand to the sea's edge in her bathing costume. She steps into the thrilling cold water. It shocks her from the ankles up, and she starts to run. The water flashes up all around her and she lifts herself to dive, and in the sun and the swing of her body she thinks an innate, almost cellular prayer: *May we never lose this.*

Lying on her back in the water she looks down the beach to see how far she has come, the Rock looming in her mind, ridged and red like some mammoth sea creature's back. In the distance the house faces the waves, white and open. She gets out of the water and walks on the sand, towards the end of the beach. In the shade she grasps a sapling trunk and pulls herself up onto the stone that marks the beginning of a steep track into the bush.

The encyclopaedia is studded with short pieces on what the writers imagine to be separate aspects of the Australian national character, its culture. Sporting Life. The Lingo. Australia as a deck of playing cards.

She reads of the bush and disappearance, of McCubbin's painting, of people found in the outback by black trackers; real-life stories turned into myth. There are rumours of missing children, local newspaper reports through the nineteenth and twentieth centuries tracking suspicious vanishings. And macabre discoveries – like that of a baby's bones found in a hidden bushland grave in a remote part of western Victoria, now a monastery's land.

To Australians the bush is a dangerous, mysterious place, she reads.

She passes over these pages and onto other mythologies, of bushrangers, or explorers. But the idea of an abandoned dead child, lying in the earth as if grown there, stays with her for days. And the absurdity of monks in Australia still strikes her, though she knows the country's history is speckled with gaggles of religious men from Europe. Like those Spanish monsignors walking the highway in their black habits under the blasting West Australian sun until the Lord told them to stop, to offer sugar and Communion to the blacks, and call that raw place New Norcia.

But the Victorian story is quieter. She cannot dislodge the image of robed men working in paddocks while up in the bush behind them is the silent, unvisited grave of a baby, lost to the bush but found by God.

Martin, too, reads these pages where they lie over the breakfast table. He thinks of the hissing bush and the buried baby. Presumably, if the story is true, it was a farmer's child. Perhaps an illegitimate child, a stillborn baby illicitly buried. The Catholics say it is a sin to bury a child unbaptised. On the drive to the city Martin is visited by the image of two pairs of parental arms lowering a small dead baby into the inhospitable earth. And what would they have done then, when this most intimate act was finished? Gone home and sat heavily in a hot farmhouse waiting for a kettle to boil? Or dropped to their knees and prayed to the hurtling sun, for any god must surely now be impossible.

Something in his doctor's self lurches at the extremity of the act, of hiding your own dead child in a secret grave. At the admission of guilt in it.

It is so warm they have begun to live at the outdoor table, eating all their meals there, reading, smoking after dinner and watching out at the waves while the insects flit against the windows.

Through this early summer Martin gives Jocelyn fishing lessons, rowing lessons, sea lessons, concocting stinking buckets of bait outside the shed. Under the watching eyes of the locals he teaches her about the tides, brings her back a pocketful of shells from each walk or fishing trip, collected from Pittwater's shallow beaches. He brings limpets, kelp snails, periwinkles and pippies. She takes them in her open palms and lets them fall clattering onto the glass porch table, their sleek undersides catching the light. Then she sweeps them with a cupped side of her hand into a bucket she keeps by the door.

And over the weeks Jocelyn gives Martin piano lessons. She spent a childhood in dark rooms with nuns holding a ruler above her fingers, and she seldom plays any longer. But at nights in this house she teaches him the left hand of Satie's *Gymnopédie No. 1*. She sits beside him on the piano stool, and slowly he plays the repeated bass line, its even, steady steps over and over, while her right hand wanders the treble notes, its lightness and movement becoming one of her walks around this island, hesitating, beginning again, losing her way and recovering it.

Alone during the days, in breaks from her work, Jocelyn sits cross-legged on the porch, reading letters from Ellen forwarded from the mountains house. She tries to picture Ellen's baby, now a small girl who Ellen says never stops talking. From here there is nothing so remote as the English winter, the Thames.

Before I came here I never knew the river was so tidal, writes

Ellen. *It makes you think that you might be near the ocean. But never an ocean like Australia's.*

Sometimes Cassandra just stares at me with this look. It's not a child's smile at all. She holds a doll dangling by the hair and our eyes meet, and she gives me this calm, superior sort of look, staring me down. Thomas, of course, thinks I'm just being dramatic.

At Ellen's wedding Jocelyn had danced with Thomas. His fingers had touched her waist, though until then their most intimate closeness had been to sit beside each other in a car, or to pass a cup or dish across a table.

But Jocelyn mostly remembers Thomas as the West Wyalong sheep farmer's boy who had seduced Ellen away from home to Sydney. Ellen would tell her, on visits home, how on the night he proposed Thomas took her to a jazz bar, leading her through the smoky sunken room to dance. How, on that blue night she said she would remember always, when the hollow trumpet note swooped clean above their heads to the ceiling beams, and Thomas had his hands on her hips, and the moon hung over the oily harbour, she said she knew it was time to take a step into her future and reach out her hand for what lay there. And she leapt for it.

Ellen's stories were always about the leaping, about the thrill of risk.

Thomas had a quick ear for music and a hankering for the unknowable things that might lie across the oceans, across the spinning globe's blue pleats, away from the sheep and the mutterings of his brother and father beneath the flattening sun. And he had rocked Ellen's body safely against his on the ship all across that wide sea to Southampton.

But once, before they were married, when Jocelyn visited Sydney, Thomas had given her a marijuana cigarette and sat back watching while she winced and hiccupped. Then they had giggled, sniggering together on the couch while Ellen sat apart, smoothly watching them now and again from her book.

At the wedding, though, they were all formality again, they were groom and bridesmaid, and Ellen sat smoothly watching them from the bridal table, surrounded by glassware and cousins.

In the evenings Martin trudges up the beach to fish for an hour before dinner. Jocelyn watches him walk on the sand, in one hand a small newspaper parcel of bait, in the other the rod pointing ahead of him, its end lifting and falling on the offbeat of each step. Sometimes in the movement of his body, holding tightly to the parcel and the rod, in his careful walk she can see him as that five-year-old boy who knew for certain that he'd cured a bird.

The sea is flat, and across the quiet water Lion Island looms.

Four

WHEN ELLEN'S BABY was born Jocelyn had visited England. They had wheeled the pram along the grey Thames, Ellen pointing and explaining, and Jocelyn had longed for the hard light of home.

Ellen was the guide, the one who knew.

Once, aged five and eight, they were walking home from the shops. Ellen said, 'We'll go a new way.' They were stopped on a corner, a stone ledge covered in pigface beside them. From here it was always two blocks until they turned left, and one block further until their white letterbox, stark against the hedge. But now Ellen stood in the sun, gesturing up an unknown street, her dress red against the fleshy fingers of the pigface and the grey stones.

Jocelyn looked up the street, shook her head. This corner was as familiar to her as her own shoes: the two houses, their lawns and wire fences. But beyond this spot, the street was another world. It stretched forever uphill, houses pale with strangeness on either side. Over the crest of that hill could be anything. Ocean, jungle, desert.

She turned back to Ellen, already feeling the moistness on her scalp.

'We'll get lost,' she said.

'For Christ's sake,' said Ellen, shaking her head, pity in her voice.

They were not allowed to swear. But Ellen's dress shouted, her plaits were straight, she was tall there in the bright afternoon and she swore. She stared at Jocelyn, her hands on her hips. Jocelyn felt her own wrong body, her thin legs, her brown boy's hair prickling at her neck. She looked up the street again, squinting into the sun towards the crest of the hill.

Ellen wanted oceans, jungles. 'You're so weak,' she said. 'I'm going this way.'

And she turned and walked up the hill, unafraid, past the new houses, past their windows flashing.

Jocelyn's face was hot, her head hurt with trying not to cry as the panic rose, as Ellen walked away up that hill to her new life in the jungle.

'Please,' she called. But Ellen's plaits swung and grew smaller until she disappeared over the hill.

Jocelyn sat in the pigface on the ledge, trying to breathe. But a noise, a door opening in the house above sent her starting off the ledge. Her feet stepped.

You know the way, she repeated in her head as she took each familiar step.

She walked. Past the starry tree with its usual red leaves. Past the dark green letterbox, past the roses. As always she crossed the next road, heart pounding, looking wildly for cars. She reached the house with the painted red driveway, began to breathe easier. One and a half blocks. You know the way.

But then a dog came running: a mud-coloured streak from the side of her vision, and the air cracking; its strained eyes and a fleck of spit landing warm on her cheek. The squeaks of the wire straining, the dog hurling itself to break through the fence as she ran, the animal beside her along the fence-line, snarling, the air turning bloody with what it would do to her, her own shrieks sucked into all the murderous noise. And over it a man's voice shouting, 'RUN, RUN!' and cackling. The fence straining – the teeth – she felt the animal's breath. Sobbing, running and running along the streets until the white flag of the letterbox was there to save her.

Her breathing wild, snot running, howling in through the gate. And at the kitchen steps there was

Ellen sitting, sucking an ice-block. She stood up when she saw Jocelyn, held out her arms. Jocelyn ran into them and Ellen held her while she sobbed out the dog and its rage. Ellen said nothing, sucking on her ice-block over Jocelyn's shoulder.

Then she said, 'I told you to come my way. I knew that dog was there.'

And she held out the colourless stump of her ice-block to Jocelyn.

Jocelyn held the ice dripping in her fingers, and listened to Ellen banging the flywire door into the kitchen, and she understood for the first time that Ellen knew the way, and that a decision without Ellen meant the world held no safe place.

From her daily walks in the bush now Jocelyn brings back twigs and sprigs and leaves, spreading them along the kitchen bench. In the manuscript she finds the flora maps with their swatches of colour, poring over them when she should be marking up the copy.

After dinner one night they drink brandy and she begins to talk to Martin about this country's plants, their shapes and habitats. He listens, exhales a long feather of cigarette smoke. When she pauses, he taps ash, nods for more. 'Keep going.'

In her mild intoxication the lacework of her thinking loosens; his nods make her brave. So she starts to tell him, almost whispering now, of an idea she's had lingering in her mind: a huge, elaborate garden of wild Australian plants. Not yet even half-imagined, but still this ludicrous ambition has begun to stay with her through her days. She is not a gardener, knows nothing of plants. She cannot believe she is voicing any part of this subliminal, impossible idea she has not even let herself properly think. But Martin keeps nodding, and she keeps talking.

He listens, watching her face, imagining with her this spiky, flowering place. 'It's beautiful,' he says, looking not at her now but out to the sea where she is planting Gymea lilies, the crimson *Doryanthes excelsa*, whose first flower appears when it's a decade old.

She's telling him things he doesn't know, but there's something familiar in her halting words – and then he recognises it. The notion of the garden. It's his own five-year-old's epiphany, and the root of his connection to her: they both can see beyond what is.

She repeats the plant names like prayers. *Eucalyptus macrocarpa. Acacia longifolia. Telopea speciosissima, Doryphora sassafras, Banksia spinulosa.* They look out at the black sea and he listens to her laying down the bones of her half-formed, holy, fantastical plan.

That night they both dream in plants, of her fingers becoming green runners and her blood turning chloro-phyllic.

The next evening he hands her a heavy parcel from Dymocks. She unwraps the paper and holds the enormous book in her two hands. *Botanica Australis*. Plants of Australia.

'For your garden,' he says.

And in this moment she knows he is the only one.

In the morning she is up before him, reading the book on the verandah as he kisses her and leaves for work. She looks up and can see him at the jetty, stepping onto the ferry, black bag dangling. He is always the last to get on board, and once there makes his way to the back as the ferry turns around, churning water. He stands in the sun and she can see him leaning over the railing, looking across the silver water to the shore. She watches until he blurs and the ferry disappears from view.

The manuscript lies open on the table, but she pushes it away to make room for the book. She spends the day turning its pages, staring at the photographs, reading, reading.

But before Martin comes home that afternoon a letter has arrived, addressed in Ellen's scrawly blue hand.

Jocelyn sits on the verandah watching the Barrenjoey headland in the fading light.

Martin swings his bag on his walk along the sandy track, up the steps, sees her face.

'Ellen is coming home,' she says.

He leans on the verandah rail, waiting to understand her small voice.

'I have to go back to the mountains,' she says. He can hardly hear her.

On the table the letter lies open like something on fire. Ellen is coming home, bringing her small daughter, leaving her husband, and three months pregnant.

Five

M R HO STANDS in his singlet, leaning slightly, breathing heavily while Martin listens to his lungs. The man's shoulders and arms are hard-muscled from years of fast and flaming work in Chinatown kitchens. Uncomplaining, but never quite comprehending Martin's words, Mr Ho has watched, then followed Martin's gestures to stand, remove his shirt, bare his back, take a deep breath, exhale, then again.

Under the stethoscope his breathing is almost normal, a little crackled. As if for luck, Martin rests his hands on Mr Ho's tawny skin for a moment while he thinks, then pulls the man's white singlet down for him. Something is not right.

Mr Ho dresses, moves to sit again, coughing into his chest.

Martin chats brightly as he writes the prescription. 'Bronchitis. Bad chest,' he says, patting his own chest. Mr Ho nods slowly at each syllable, takes the paper from Martin.

Once he has left Martin's doorway there's a yelp from the receptionist, Susan, a young woman who wears black eyeliner and her blonde hair piled high on her head. Martin steps through to see Mr Ho holding out a wooden box to Susan.

That evening as Martin drives through the city, across the bridges and north along the coast road, he knows suddenly it is not bronchitis that has hold of Mr Ho's breathing. He wants to turn the car around immediately. The wheeze, and that uneasy space in his own certainty when he lifted his hands from Mr Ho's skin, have moved and wavered in the back of his mind since, and now the pattern has cleared. Tomorrow he will get Susan to write to Mr Ho and call him back in, order an X-ray. It is early enough. Not all omens are bad ones.

His headlights wash the road pale, and the eucalyptus leaves glitter as he drives.

Tomorrow Jocelyn is leaving Pittwater for the mountains.

They have argued about it. Ellen was a grown woman, could surely look after herself, he'd said. And Jocelyn was a grown woman too, not a servant.

'But she's my sister,' Jocelyn said, looking out of the window to the sea.

And then he had said (so *stupid*, he knows it), 'If we were married I could forbid you.' Hated himself even as the words came out, as he stood by the mantelpiece picking at the paint with his fingernail. But they were there, in the air.

Jocelyn stood up, and met his eyes. 'Yes,' she said. 'Perhaps that's why we're not.' And she went into the bedroom to begin packing her things.

An animal's eyes flash from the undergrowth in his headlights. He jams the brakes, but it disappears.

It is not forever, she said more than once, after his apologies. So. He will travel up to the mountains as he has before, on weekends. Will talk to George about more locum work.

Not all omens are bad.

When he reaches home he leads her, covering her eyes, to the kitchen, and then uncovers them to see the live mud crab, stunned and shifting against the sides of the sink. Two hand-spans across, bronze, slow and prehistoric. It was in Mr Ho's newspaper-lined apple box on the back seat of the car all the way back from the city, its great pincers bound tightly to itself with brown string, the wiry antennae searching and bending. Then on the ferry, the odd other passenger coming to stare into the box beside him and give a little shriek at the moving dark mass.

Now in the kitchen he and Jocelyn drink riesling while he tells, laughing, about Mr Ho trying to give the crab to Susan, the man's bewilderment at her horrified squeal. Mr Ho told him how to cook it, gestured how to kill it first, with chopsticks, but Martin thinks the knife steel will do it. The animal shunts in the sink. Martin talks on, how the pincers could break your fingers, how the crabs are caught with poles in the oozing suck and pop of the mangroves.

Neither of them says anything about tomorrow.

Jocelyn walks out to the sand's edge to watch the last ferry come in while he crashes about in the kitchen, swearing. She goes back in once during the procedure; the great creature has a bunch of tea towel viced in one pincer. Martin hoists the towel and the crab hangs there, unmoving. Martin's giggle is unconvincing. He holds a long kitchen knife in his other hand. Jocelyn goes back out to the porch and watches the ferry passengers wheelbarrowing their supplies through the moonlight away from the beach, torches bobbing. The ferry heaves away from the wharf, whirling water.

An hour and a half later they sit, with large dinner plates and the nutcracker, at the porch table in the lamplight to eat. Martin is flush-faced, and insects tap in quiet circles against the house.

The moon is up. The white humps of the upturned boats glow violet in the sand at the edges of the lawns and the water moves like oil, slapping at the beach. In the bedroom Jocelyn's suitcase lies packed, *Botanica Australis* wrapped in a petticoat underneath her clothes.

Before eating, they talk about her trip back to her sister, as if it's a weekend away. They speak brightly about the road, how the neighbours who had reluctantly accepted the dog will be happy to give him back, about airing out the house. But as Martin listens to her voice as she talks about Ellen he feels some part of her confidence faltering, some child's timidity emerging in her.

They sit in the lamplight, eating. After the first exclamations and overworked smiles – Jocelyn toasts Martin and his crab in a too-loud voice – they fall into silence and eat doggedly, passing utensils back and forth, the cracking of the creature's skin sounding out across the sand and the waves.

On Jocelyn's second weekend of the long-ago visit to England the sun had come out.

They had driven to Cambridge through the summer morning, and Jocelyn had never felt such soft light on her skin. The three of them stood on the bridge, leaning over, looking down at the punts. The water glimmered and there was quiet laughter and the knock of poles against the wooden boats.

'Let's have a go,' Thomas had said. Ellen rolled her eyes.

Jocelyn held out her arms for the baby. 'You two go, I'll take Cassandra. It'll be romantic.'

But Ellen shook her head. 'It'll be time to feed her, she'll scream.' She paused, watching Jocelyn and Thomas, then said, 'You two go.'

Jocelyn began to say no, but Thomas said to Ellen, 'You'll be all right, won't you? Come on, Joss,' and was down the stairs talking to one of the boater-hatted attendants.

The attendant held Jocelyn's arm while she stepped into the flat-bottomed boat. Ellen watched from the bridge, and Jocelyn waved to her and the baby.

Thomas clambered in, took the pole from the man.

'Let's show these bloody poms how it's done then, eh Joss,' he said, his voice unchanged but suddenly so Australian, and he flexed a bicep, and they both laughed when he leaned heavily on the pole and groaned, barely moving the boat an inch from the pontoon.

'Jesus bloody Christ,' he said through gritted teeth as the punt edged away in the wrong direction. Jocelyn turned to wave again at Ellen, and laugh with her at Thomas's wobbling and grunting.

Then the boat turned, Thomas managed a good shove, and they moved smoothly towards the arched bridge. He looked up, blew a kiss to Ellen and the baby, and called out, 'Half an hour.'

Ahead of them downstream, clutches of students lounged in the boats as if they lived in them. One punt glided past, two pale girls lying back sleepily on cushions and blankets, sipping champagne. A young man in a green shirt rested his weight on one hip at the end of the boat, pole in one hand, steering effortlessly through the willow-shadowed water.

Thomas, swearing and grunting, managed with great effort to begin using the pole as a rudder. 'How do those bastards do it and look like that?' he grunted, scowling.

Jocelyn smiled. 'Do you want me to help?'

'Of course not. I was a frigging surf life-saver, remember.'

They both snorted, both knowing he had not been, and Jocelyn turned and lounged, watching the other boats drift, or occasionally circle clumsily like theirs, stuck against one another under one of the narrow stone bridges.

On either side of the stone embankments stretched the vast, luminous lawns.

Then Thomas had the hang of it and manoeuvred the boat without looking, and Jocelyn watched him through half-closed eyes, a silhouette of beauty against that river of green.

Suddenly at a bend in the river, Kings College rose into view, all pale stone grandeur. It loomed higher and higher until it was right in front of them, and Jocelyn knew she would never forget this moment, this gliding by England's dreaming architecture under her pale-blue summer sky.

Fifty minutes later they could hear the baby's wails before they reached the last bridge, and scrambling from the boat onto the pontoon they saw Ellen, walking up and down the bridge, jostling and jogging the baby.

'Shit,' murmured Thomas, 'we're in for it.'

None of them spoke in the car on the way home. Ellen was totally silent, staring out at the road ahead while Jocelyn sat in the back, patting at Cassandra under the blankets wound tightly around her in the carry cot, her small red face whitening across the nose as she screamed. Until, eventually exhausted, she fell into sleep, still breathing now and again with a deep shudder.

On this Pittwater morning the beach is rimmed with a lace of crushed white shell. Martin lifts her suitcase from the jetty into the room of the boat and they board together. The other passengers don't look, careful to turn their gaze anywhere but at *the doctor's woman* leaving. Jocelyn and Martin watch their house and the beach moving away. She watches Lion Island as Martin tells her again that he will see her in a couple of weeks.

After he's helped load her things into her car – the manuscript in its rubber-banded parcels on the front seat – they kiss there in the gravel car park. His hands rest on her hips until the ferry horn sounds for its return trip. Only then does he walk across the gravel to his car. She starts her engine and then he turns his own key, and they each sit, waiting for the engines to warm, watching the ferry in its lumbering turn towards their beach, their summer.

It moves away over that now uncrossable swathe of water.

Six

S HE WALKS THROUGH the cold house in the mountains, drawing back the heavy curtains, trying to
imagine the baby Cassandra now a child.

She drags furniture into the old glasshouse, their
father's private pottering place. In the evening light the
air is pale green.

The glasshouse walls are cement as high as the waist,
glass panes above. At the base of the window a wooden
shelf a foot wide runs the length of all four walls, lined
with terracotta pots, buckets, knives. Under the shelf,
against the concrete wall, are the water pipes once mildly
heated from a wood stove at the back of the building.
A stool has been dragged up to a potting table. She's
installed a battered kerosene heater nearby; garden tools
are piled in a corner. Down the centre of the glasshouse
is a long trestle table, piled with other paraphernalia: seed

trays, a trowel, cardboard pieces, a pen, dirty ice-cream sticks, wire, a sack of old fertiliser.

She sets out her reference books and the manuscript on the desk which she has dragged out from the house, then lugs in the box of books she's brought back from Pittwater, and the other things, the pressed plant cuttings from the bush, their sticky-tape labels. Some small rough drawings that might be part of a garden, the wad of dried sea kelp and the bucket of shells. On one of the glass walls she sticks pictures of plants, drawings, botanical illustrations from magazines and books. In front of this wall of buckling paper she piles other things. She pushes in the broken office chair, its back swung sideways on the metal frame.

She lifts out the book Martin gave her, puts it on the trestle table, making a place for herself for when Ellen arrives.

When they were children Ellen would drag the tangled coils of the garden hose to the front lawn and position the sprinkler and its triangular upward fan of water. Then she would stand a little way off, holding a length of hose and bending it hard to cut off the water supply to the sprinkler. Then she started the countdown, and at nought Jocelyn would sprint from the corner near the fence, diagonally across the grass, to the opposite corner. Her leap over the sprinkler was Ellen's cue – she would snap the hose straight and send the water shooting up again. Then it was Jocelyn's turn to hold the hose; whoever remained driest at the end of the game was the victor.

Jocelyn was the quicker, more accurate judge of the movement of water in the plastic hose, and in the first minutes of the game Ellen dripped while Jocelyn's clothes were almost completely dry. Ellen's face began to darken after each slippery grass landing, pushing back wet hair from her face. Not squealing after the first three turns, just concentrating hard when it was her turn for the hose in her hand, as Jocelyn began her run-up.

And Jocelyn knew the unspoken rules as well.

So from then on she made a silent game of her own. She timed her leap to match Ellen's releasing of the hose, calibrating the movement in her legs as she had done with the hose in her hand, slowing or speeding at the last second, never taking her eyes from Ellen's fingers. Awarding herself points at each of Ellen's triumphant shrieks and crows, giving herself a star for every perfect soaking.

She won her secret game every time, and Ellen hooted with delight at her sister's dripping hair and her footprints on the porch as they went inside for lunch.

That night Martin's voice is lively on the telephone, talking about a lorry driver with a death wish on the road home from the city. Jocelyn twists the black plastic coil around her fingers and pictures him in the house, folded into the cherry-coloured armchair with his long legs dangling over its side, rubbing his forehead as he speaks. She wants to walk past and touch his pale, fine hair.

She tells him about the new letter from Ellen. She will arrive on the third, did not answer Jocelyn's questions. *I'll tell you everything when I get there*, Ellen had written. Ellen still decides the rules.

Jocelyn hangs up, returns to the lamplit glasshouse and the manuscript, to Lake Eyre, the inland sea. *At the edge of three deserts in the middle of the continent, it is the lowest point of Australia's geography.* She reads that the place is itself another low desert, where only once in the past century the enormous lake has formed, the rising water nine times as salty as the ocean. Once or twice a century the earth lique-fies, shimmering, spreading outwards into the stillness. The gravitational pull of the moon forms tides on the water, and life begins to flicker and slide and crawl and stagger from the shallows. And from thousands and thousands of miles away, the birds come. Over the water, the budgerigar and the cockatiel: a vast, brilliant sheet of screaming air.

Jocelyn spends the next days working on the manuscript, tidying the yard, cleaning the house, setting out rat traps in the laundry. Ellen is leaving Thomas, will not say why. In the evenings Jocelyn writes to or telephones Martin. One night she takes a page and scribbles a glimpse of an imaginary garden.

She cleans spider webs and hauls mouldy blankets out from the old kennel for Alf, who is bewildered but happily home again after the months with a neighbour. He stomps the perimeter of the garden, sniffing and pissing.

Jocelyn makes up the bed for Cassandra in Ellen's childhood room, sticking coloured pictures on the walls and collecting their old toys from boxes and cupboards, washing them, combing the dolls' matted hair, sitting them on the bed in welcome. But when she passes by the door she sees them there, leached of their colours, the ragged bears and the dolls cracked, tired out from all the years.

And as Jocelyn shops for food – avoiding the glances of people she knows have heard about her going away with Martin – and hangs meat in the meat house, arranges for firewood to be delivered, chops kindling, it is as though she is still their father's maid, as though he had not died years ago, as though she had never left.

Or as though she is their mother, in those years before she died, constantly moving through the house, mapping it with her dusting rags, or on her knees scrubbing, as if she could scour her marriage clean. The more their father stayed away from home, the more their mother scrubbed and starched and ironed. When he came back it was worse, his infidelities carried in the air around him like the cling of tobacco smoke. Jocelyn remembers the taut dinners, the sound of crockery knocking in the sink, her mother bent over it, holding dishes under the water as if to drown them. She remembers Ellen, at sixteen, shouting at their mother in a distant room – *Why do you put* UP *with it!*

Once, after Jocelyn gave the engagement ring back to the boy, her mother accused her in the hallway: 'A marriage doesn't have to be perfect. You make the best of things.'

Jocelyn rakes leaves in the garden, cuts the grass, sweeps the verandah, and tries to remember how Martin stood on this front step and changed everything.

Martin switches the porch light on before he closes the front door behind him in the mornings now. He cannot stand the darkness of the house across the sand when he gets off the ferry. After he reads Jocelyn's letters, or speaks to her, he takes a fishing rod and his cigarettes and goes to sit in the dark on the jetty. Sometimes he stays there until the morning.

Seven

AND NOW SUDDENLY one new November morning it is Ellen standing on that step, saying, 'Of course, I thought you knew.'

Arriving from the train station, suitcase in one hand and a small girl's white hand in the other. The stylish cut of Ellen's bone-coloured jacket over her shoulders there on the porch, her perfectly polished, unscuffed shoes. And Cassandra, a tiny, puppy-fat version of her mother, in navy trousers and a cream viyella blouse, the two of them emotionless against the hard sunlight and the gash of red azalea.

Thomas has always hit her, Ellen says. 'Especially during pregnancies.'

Suddenly all Jocelyn can think of is Ellen's immeasurable kindness in those nights when Jocelyn was four and the nightmare came again – that dark and undulating force, *monster* too trivial a word even then for the evil of its vast, curtainous mass. Ellen would bring her little sister into her own bed, wriggle them both so as to untangle their flannel nightgowns, and hold close around Jocelyn's chubby waist from behind. Ellen would kiss the back of her head, wearily whisper to her to *think of nice things, remember the beach? Your blue dress?* And cradle her back to sleep. Daytime restored them to squabbles over hair ribbons and Ellen's complicated rules, but at night, at seven years old, Ellen was her staunchest guardian.

And now it is Jocelyn's turn.

Ellen's matter-of-factness. 'Did you never wonder why after all this time we only had one child? I had two miscarriages because of it.'

Jocelyn turns from the front door, gesturing them to sit, walking through treacle to the kitchen. The leaden teapot.

Thomas has always hit Ellen.

When Jocelyn returns to the dining room Cassandra is staring out the window at the ragged mess of the eucalypts and the failed, patchy lawn. Ellen sits in the green leather armchair with its springs prolapsing to the floor beneath, and Jocelyn is overwhelmed by the inadequacy of anything she has to offer. She cannot stop her tears coming.

Ellen jumps up and pulls Jocelyn to her, smoothing her spine, calming her, clucking away her shame at needing comfort when she should be offering protection. Ellen whispers, *It's all right, it's finished, we're home now, it's finished.* This time is different, she's left for good, she has money, she's home. She will have the baby here and everything will be all right.

Jocelyn straightens and leans to touch Cassandra's hair. The little girl, dry-eyed, does not look up, but keeps chewing the mouthful of Milk Arrowroot biscuit she's taken from the opened packet and watches a sulphur-crested cockatoo waddle like an old white dog across the garden.

That night Ellen tucks Sandra into bed, telling her stories about the dolls Jocelyn has put out and reading from one of their childhood fairytale books. Later Jocelyn lies in her bed across the hall, listening to Ellen unpacking in their parents' room. Her mind fills with images of Thomas, winking at her across a dinner table, rolling his eyes about Ellen, at Cambridge. *She's so melodramatic.* And then into her mind comes the other, unbearable image: on Ellen's wrist when she took off her jacket today, a pale but definite pink line, straight as a pencil. 'Oh, just an old scar,' she had said, and pulled her sleeve down again.

Martin arrives at the end of the week. As Jocelyn fills the kettle she hears Martin and Ellen talking with an ease she has never had with her own sister. They are discussing Ellen's pregnancy.

Jocelyn goes outside to look for Sandra, finds her squatting near the woodshed over a terracotta flower pot in which she has trapped four snails and is filling the pot with bits of grass and leaves.

'Would you like a piece of cake, Sandra?' Jocelyn asks, squatting down beside her.

Sandra says nothing, does not look up, but shakes her head. Peering into the pot.

Jocelyn pulls a few blades of grass from a tuft near her foot and offers it to her. 'Is this the right sort of grass?'

Sandra takes the little bunch, looks at it closely. 'No,' she says, and passes it back to Jocelyn. She takes it and tosses it aside.

'How many snails have you got there?'

Sandra meets her gaze for a second. She is dark-haired like her mother, her skin pale with Englishness. But where Ellen's eyes are green Sandra's are dark brown, like Jocelyn's.

'Twelve,' she says.

'I see,' nods Jocelyn, shifting to sit cross-legged on the ground beside her. She wants to reach out and touch Sandra's hand, but resists the urge.

'This one's called Jeremy,' breathes Sandra, pointing with a stick at one snail stuck three-quarters up the pot's side, slowly making for escape. Her voice has an adult clarity and volume Jocelyn has never heard in the muffled, mumbled speech of Australian children. 'No you don't,' says Sandra sweetly, and wields her stick to flick Jeremy from the side and clack him roughly back into the pot.

When Jocelyn returns to the dining room Ellen and Martin are smiling at her.

'Martin's going to deliver the baby,' Ellen says, beaming.

Ellen's first check-up is 'like playing doctors and nurses'; she giggles, making her face prim and walking haughtily. Martin is playful too, ushering her into the surgery, pretending not to know her, calling her *Madam*.

While he peels back her sleeve and wraps the black rubber cuff around her upper arm Ellen looks around and jokes there should be Van Gogh's sunflowers, isn't that what doctors' rooms always have?

Martin puffs the little ball in his hand. The band tightens on her skin. He stops, examines the dial, and then lets out the band with a sound of released air. As the air hisses he says, 'So what exactly has happened, injury-wise?'

She leans back for a moment, closes her eyes, then opens them. 'Do we really have to go into this?'

He says, merely, softly, 'Yes.'

So Ellen begins talking, in a shopping-list voice, sometimes lifting her blouse or standing and turning, pulling her skirt away from her back for him to see, chronicling the years of damage done to her body in another country on the other side of the world.

Martin watches her while she speaks, and listens, and thinks about other, invisible kinds of pain.

In the night Martin climbs out of the fold-out bed in the sun-room where he sleeps now that Sandra and Ellen are here, and goes to Jocelyn's room. They touch each other's skin, and whisper the news of their week into the dark.

'Sandra reminds me of me when I was little,' she says. 'All that silence and staring.'

He strokes her hand where he holds it flat on his chest. 'Poor little you,' he says.

He has talked to George, who has given him a day's locum work on Mondays, and the Sydney practice will let him have the extra day away.

Jocelyn presses her fingers on her closed eyes, hard, in the dark to stop herself from crying. She knows she should be pleased. It's an extra night. But she wants him never to leave.

They talk softly through the hours, until they fall asleep. Jocelyn pretends she can hear the sea outside.

Ellen plumps cushions, takes possession of the house as she moves through the rooms. 'Thank God we had you to come home to,' she says to Jocelyn one afternoon when the sun through the window divides the living room into quarters. Jocelyn nods, thinking of the way the sun strikes water, not glass. Thinking of Martin, of the meanings of home.

Among the belongings Ellen puts around the house are her photographs in frames. She has several of her bridal ship journey with Thomas to England. She and Thomas in fancy-dress, a pharaoh king and queen. She had been skilful with their makeup and gold lamé. His eyes are particularly accentuated, pencilled black and sensuous into wide cat's corners, and he has golden card-board epaulettes on his shoulders and manacles on his wrists. It sickens Jocelyn now to see the picture, but Ellen is somehow buoyed by it; she can make the distinction in time, can separate the resting power in Thomas's hands from what happened later. Not much later, though, she says thoughtfully – the last port of call had been memor-able for their first exquisite argument, his dizzying shove of her against the cabin door. She had been drunk, and therefore could see that she had perhaps brought it on herself, and they apologised to each other, crying, for days.

In the photograph Thomas's hands are large, his fingers curved, not threateningly, over Ellen's honey shoulders.

She wears a golden serpent coiled around her throat, and its head, having slithered up the nape of her neck and up through the high nest of her curling black hair, descends again to rest like a jewel in the centre of her forehead. She laughs now, holding the photograph. 'It took me days and *God* knows how many tins of gold paint and yards of tinfoil, that wretched snake!'

The serpent's little malevolent eyes were a pair of marcasite earrings, a gift from Thomas.

In other pictures from that voyage she is voluptuous and sleep-eyed under sun hats so broad they fill the frame. The photographs are black-and-white, but Jocelyn always sees her sister in red.

Though it is early November Ellen has insisted that Sandra go to school in the town for the weeks until Christmas. She bossed the headmaster into it in a short meeting, her loud English voice sounding around his little office, and now she or Jocelyn walks Sandra to the school gates in the mornings and waits there for her again in the afternoons.

Jocelyn took her there on the first day. Sandra held Jocelyn's hand tightly, gripping the hard plastic handle of the brown Globite school case in her other hand. Jocelyn saw two boys turn and stare at Sandra, hands on their grey serge hips, waiting to see what she would do when Jocelyn let go her hand. Jocelyn remembered stepping onto the ferry at Palm Beach. She asked Sandra if she was all right, but the girl did not answer, only tilted her face to be kissed as Jocelyn bent down. Then she let go her aunt's hand and walked steadily past the two staring boys, into that bright square of playground and monkey-bars and other children's noise.

A week later Jocelyn is trimming quail in the kitchen, and Sandra comes to stand beside her, watching the cleaver come down to crush and snap the thin birdy bones. The halved, pink-fleshed bodies lie slumped in a heap to one side. 'Out of the way, Sandra, I don't want to hurt you,' Jocelyn says. It is the violence she does not want the girl to see. She tries to cut more quietly, but the bones won't break, so she returns to the sharp, heavy dropping of the cleaver, trying to put her body between Sandra and the bones. But Sandra moves to get a better view, concentrating, interested. After a time she says, in a casual, adult's voice, 'Is that lobster?'

Jocelyn almost drops the knife, but is careful not even to smile.

'No, sweetheart, it's quail. Little birds, like chickens.'

'Oh,' says Sandra, disappointed. She pushes hair from her eyes and then wanders outside to find the dog.

The mind of a child, the endless acceptance of new,

unthinkable things. Like finding yourself on the other side of the world in a land where the bark of the trees is red and you have been let go by a father who swore you were his most loved thing.

Sandra carries everywhere with her now a feeble picture book Jocelyn had bought for her during their first days here when Sandra had hardly spoken. The story involves a kangaroo's joey lost in an unfamiliar part of the bush where it doesn't belong, and finding its way home by asking for help from other tedious national symbols: koala, echidna, wombat, lyrebird. All first hostile at the junior outsider's intrusions and too busy to help, what with their sleeping, digging, snuffling and tail-spreading to do, but then charmed into taking pity in the dark bush on the poor, lost, child marsupial. Even a cranky-then-kindly brown snake – somehow perching up like a rattlesnake in the illustration – hisses some advice. In the final scene the joey leaps across two pages into its mother's waiting pouch.

After hearing Ellen read it aloud Jocelyn remembers the lost-child rumours from the encyclopaedia, and the buried baby. Something about it makes her want to rip the book from her niece's hands. She is worried about the ideas she has begun to plant in her, of being lost, of foreignness. But

Sandra, glossy head bent, pores over the thing constantly in corners of the house and garden, murmuring the names of these alien animals quietly to herself.

'It's only a book, Joss,' Ellen soothes. 'She loves it.'

Jocelyn watches Ellen through the days, hears her sharp voice ordering Sandra about. Now and then Ellen puts two hands on her swelling belly. Jocelyn begins to feel consumed by anxiety for these new lost children, born and unborn.

Martin helps Jocelyn in the vegetable garden, tying the slender stems of tomatoes to wooden stakes. It is two weeks since Ellen and Sandra arrived.

Martin has something to say. He takes a breath: 'I'm not sure about Ellen's injuries.'

It's the first truly hot midday of summer, and there is no shade in this treeless part of the garden. Jocelyn looks up at him, still tying the string. 'What do you mean?'

He is holding a green bevelled stem to the stake while she knots the string. He doesn't answer, standing there behind the plant, holding it like a line between himself and her.

She straightens, brushes hair from her hot face.

'Are you saying you don't believe her?'

He breathes in, fingers still on the whetstone silk of the stem. 'No, it's completely possible that he's hurt her. But I'm just not sure the particular things she's told me are completely accurate. She's emphasising things I just can't see, that would be more evident. And –' he pauses, watching her – 'what she said to you about miscarriages. Injury during pregnancy, unless it's late term and a really major blow, like a car accident, actually rarely results in miscarriage.'

He waits, then says, 'What I mean is, perhaps she's just making things slightly more dramatic, that's all. It's understandable.'

Jocelyn stares at him. This cool doctor's voice she has never heard. Used like a scalpel: the slight, easy pressure, drawing a fine red incision into Ellen's life. *Melodramatic.* Something violent in her flashes.

'You sound like Thomas.' She spits the words.

Martin closes his eyes. 'Look –'

'And don't you *dare* say to me, "that's all".' Her rage stuns her.

Martin says nothing now, only holds her gaze across the green lines.

And then Sandra is walking down the path between the lettuces towards them. It is the first time she has come near the two of them alone, without her mother. They both stay silent, keep still, so as not to scare away this new small creature in the garden.

Jocelyn breathes. 'Hello, sweetheart,' she murmurs.

Sandra stops, gapes at her as if at something fearful and ugly, and Jocelyn instantly regrets her familiarity.

Sandra puts a fingernail between her teeth. Martin starts working again, lifting the bowed tomato vine. Jocelyn instinctively follows him, tying the plant where he holds it, each of them careful, quiet. The sun is high. Sandra stands watching them as they work. They hear the click of her teeth on the fingernail, and she takes the torn sliver from her tongue like a hair, examines it, her dark, fine head bent in the sun. Then her voice comes, high and English among the vegetables.

'Mummy says can you please come in for lunch.'

She doesn't wait for a reply, but turns away, and they watch her stolid, rocking walk back up the path, her small legs too pale, too pale for this country's hard-hearted sun.

'Thank you, darling,' Jocelyn calls, and moves to follow her.

Martin whispers, 'Hang on,' and catches her arm. She stops but says, not looking at him, 'You're wrong. You don't understand anything about Ellen.'

He pauses, and then nods slowly. He takes her hand and holds it tight as they walk out of the garden.

Ellen has set the dining table for a proper meal. Ordinarily Jocelyn and Martin would have made a sandwich at the kitchen bench and eaten it outside on the lawn, reading or talking, uncut sandwiches spilling bits into the grass.

But today there is an ironed tablecloth, diced salad in bowls, a loaf of bread precisely sawn, rare roast beef in thin slices, mustard in little dishes. There are wine glasses, and water glasses.

'This is lovely,' Jocelyn says into the hollow room when they are seated around the table. Ellen picks up dishes and puts down her fork and swallows and talks and laughs.

Sandra has a serviette tucked in at her neck like a board and eats a sandwich in jigsaw pieces, sniffing, looking only at her plate.

Ellen is asking about Sydney, about shopping. She winks at Martin and says she's sure Jocelyn won't know where the decent shops are. In small, underneath moments Jocelyn sees Martin quietly including Sandra. He makes her smile once, is not pushy.

And all the time Ellen tinkles, tinkles across the table.

Eight

THE EUCALYPT IS EVERYWHERE. *The pungent foliage of Australia's eucalyptus trees – more than 600 species in all – create the country's most evocative aroma. The eucalypts range in size from 10 to 300 feet high, and grow everywhere from swamp to stony desert to tropical rainforest.*

Her pencil hovers over the line of type, but she can think of no words to convey that blade to the senses, that incision of the air when a gum leaf is torn. The explosive thread of scent that will one day have her heaving with homesickness.

Ellen sips cordial in the garden.

'They say you can inherit it,' she says. 'Violence, I mean.'

They are watching Sandra play with the old brown dog. Ellen's voice is smooth and unremarking. She drinks from a glass embossed with red and gold curlicues, elegant in her hand. She is made for Australian light, sitting here in the wicker garden chair, stroking her turquoise paisley blouse over her belly and setting the glass on the table. Watching her daughter, she idly twists the rose-gold wedding band on her finger.

Jocelyn sits there in the same accepting silence with which she has greeted Ellen's statements since childhood. *Ladies wear stockings. Dogs give you rabies.*

Ellen stretches out, arms backwards over her head, her narrow hips and growing belly rising to the fading sky. The blouse rides up to reveal a panel of taut, creamy skin above the shirring of her black trousers.

Sandra whoops at Alf down by the fence, flailing her arms and stepping back, making him leap higher, higher each time. The old dog, unused to such wild attention, is eager, jumping determinedly on his lumpen legs, eyes fixed on the ball in Sandra's hand, tongue lolling. A once-skilled old boxer enticed back inside the ring.

Ellen turns in her seat to follow the low flight of a magpie.

'You don't realise how much you miss these until you come back,' she says.

It is the time of the afternoon when Jocelyn used to sit out here alone, bracing herself against the birds as they gathered in the high branches of the gums. They would plummet in diagonals around her, scudding at knee height then shooting vertical to the tree, squawking and squealing as they flew. It was difficult not to take personally those carefully aimed sideswipes just above her, behind her head.

Now, spring gone into summer, with Ellen here and Sandra skidding with the dog over the lawn, the magpies meet more sedately, fluttering up and settling, dropping their double-noted calls into the air.

Jocelyn watches them closely, listens to her sister, watches her turn the wedding ring. Since Ellen came back, nothing is as it seems.

Martin drives the three hours from Sydney on Friday evenings, his headlights spreading the bush white on the winding roads. Spends a day at George's surgery in the mountains on Mondays, then leaves at dawn on Tuesday to set off again for the surgery in the city, and then there is the drive back to the beach. Even though the drive here is not so much longer than the daily one between the city and the beach house, Jocelyn is riven with guilt about all his travelling, and the mountains roads are more dangerous. She has visions of his car airborne over one of those orange cliffs, but still cannot bring herself to tell him to stay home and rest: by Friday nights his calm presence is all she wants. His warm thigh next to hers at the table, his voice gentle against Ellen's. In the dawn mists on Tuesdays she watches his car drive out into the street and tries not to feel like a visited prisoner.

Each week Ellen grows larger, her clothes tighter across the breasts and belly. One morning after they drop Sandra at school, Ellen and Jocelyn go shopping for more maternity clothes. In the town's one dress shop Ellen, half-naked in the dressing room, shrieks from behind the curtain, pokes her head out and dangles for Jocelyn a new, enormous white brassiere. Then she and Jocelyn bite their lips to stop from laughing as the shop woman, Mrs Berner, whom they have known since they were children, stands in front of Ellen, all serious work and frowning, pushing and lifting at Ellen's breasts and tugging the shoulder straps so hard that Ellen sways in the little curtained room.

Afterwards in the tea shop they snigger into their tea.

'As though she was fitting a damn horse's *bridle*,' Ellen squeals, sending them both into a fresh fit of hysteria.

Nine

JOCELYN READS OF Coober Pedy, the underground opal-mining town of South Australia, lying in a shallow dish of clay and sandstone.

She scribbles her notes, trying to push away thoughts of Ellen and Thomas.

The Coober Pedy townsfolk live in dugout rooms under the earth, to keep out of the overwhelming heat. The inhabitants, the gougers, eke out a living in the narrow mineshafts, bringing up ore by the bucketful, gouging at the walls of their corridors in the dark for the elusive seam of opal. Or, less profitably, they live from 'noodling', sorting through the discarded stone and earth with sticks for overlooked pieces of the gem.

Occasionally opal worth hundreds of thousands of pounds is found. But most people will never make their fortunes at Coober Pedy. Yet still they hope each day for the bright glimpse that will change their lives, watching for it as they climb down into the dark with explosives in their hands.

Blue letters from Thomas begin to arrive. Remorseful, self-righteous. Cassandra has the right to a father, he rages. *So does the other one.*

In 1963, women do not leave their husbands. Thomas is pitiful, shamed, wheedling, threatening. The letters are thirty pages long, or two lines. They are tender, nostalgic, paranoid, drunken. All on airmail paper, arriving in the letterbox daily at first, then in jerky spates.

Jocelyn wants to tear the letters up, take them from the letterbox and toss them straight into the incinerator. She does, once, but Ellen discovers this and becomes the most animated Jocelyn has seen her, shouting that Jocelyn has no right.

So now she hands the letters over, expressionless. Or she sees from the glasshouse – Ellen (or worse, Cassandra) reaching into the letterbox, drawing out her hand, turning the envelope over to see its handwriting. Ellen usually pockets the letter then, to read later, privately. When Jocelyn does see her reading occasionally, in the garden, something like satisfaction glimmers across her face. Sometimes it is fear. Jocelyn begins dreaming of Thomas's arrival, hair flying, grown larger and dishevelled by grief and rage, devouring them all.

But in Jocelyn's bed at night Martin whispers that the man is a coward who will take no action; that whatever he's done, he merely wants his rants. That Ellen has done the right thing, that when the baby comes she will feel safe, and Jocelyn can come back to Pittwater.

Lying in the bed with Jocelyn held curved into the cave of his body, however, Martin dreams that this is what happens: a squall over the house, a pale storm starting from the far corner of the garden, moving across the months, darkening as it nears.

Sandra swears cheerfully at the dog. 'You bastard, Alf,' she says in her high clear voice, lurching sideways from his raised leg, through the front door into the hallway gloom. Ellen hears her from the kitchen, calls, '*Sandra!*'

Jocelyn is passing with an armful of books, and she and Sandra smirk at each other, then turn, screeching their disgust, to see Alf steadying himself to shit on the front step, like a circus elephant perching on a bucket. Jocelyn kicks at the screen door, yelling 'Alf! You're revolting! *Get* away!', startling him into a stumble. He recovers, then moves awkwardly, interrupted, into the garden.

Sandra is sent to her room, and in the dining room Ellen blames Jocelyn for her daughter's vocabulary. Blames Martin, whom she has heard say 'bastard' within Sandra's earshot.

It is one of those days when Ellen's voice fills the room, upper-class and British. Jocelyn half-listens. Through the window she can see Alf now happily straining on the lawn.

'She's a child, for God's sake, Joss. And it's not funny.'

A large turd curves from the dog's flared anus. Jocelyn feels sick. She turns to stare into her tea cup, the faint oily slick of the milk reflecting the window's light.

'Sandra has been through,' Ellen is saying more quietly, breathing unevenly, 'I would think, enough. And I have bloody well been through enough without seeing my sister turn my child into a sewer-mouthed brat because I've been stupid.'

Oh, Ellen.

Ellen pulls at the blue tablecloth with her pale finger-nails. The skin on her face is beginning to lose its fineness.

Jocelyn cannot speak for guilt. 'I'm sorry,' she says, not meeting Ellen's eyes but standing to collect her sister's empty tea cup in the only gesture she can manage. She carries the cups from the room. As she passes the window she catches sight of Alf half-heartedly scuffing grass-dust over his shining faeces on the lawn.

Martin brings Sandra a cane hula hoop from Woolworths in the city, and she spends Saturday morning out on the porch with it, trying to start it swinging around her waist.

From the dining room over breakfast they watch her. She swings the hoop too hard and tries swivelling, hipless in her yellow frock, dropping her little body wildly from side to side before the hoop clatters again to the cement. 'Damn,' her small voice says.

The dog sits on the grass watching, head nodding up or down at the hoop as it is lifted and dropped.

Ellen rises from the table, appears at the porch. 'Sandra, what did I say about language?' Sandra looks up at her, squinting in the sun. Then Ellen says, 'Let me show you, darling.'

'I can do it,' Sandra says, holding the hoop at her shoulder, away from her mother's outstretched hands. Sandra catches sight of Jocelyn and Martin behind the glass of the window.

'Don't you watch me,' she shouts at Ellen, and then glares at them through the glass. They turn back to the newspaper pages.

But Ellen has hold of the hoop. 'I'm just *showing* you,' she says, 'don't be silly.'

Sandra lets it go, steps off the porch, sullen, hands stuck into her armpits. 'I don't care, I don't want to *do* it any more.'

Ellen steps into the hoop. It's a graceful movement; even pregnant, she has a dancer's slink. She holds the cane between her fingers and with a flick starts it spinning at her hips, grinning at Sandra who has dropped her arms, still angry but watching closely.

Ellen has her rhythm up, and raises her hands above her head, the hoop swivelling, swivelling beneath her belly, and she smiles into the sunshine. Sandra steps towards her, shouting 'I can do it now!' But Ellen only holds out a slim hand to keep her away, keeps moving, glances at the window where they are watching and waves, begins to giggle. Jocelyn puts down her tea cup and Martin his paper and Sandra stands, expressionless, and they all watch the sliding, off-centre rhythm of Ellen's hips and her belly and the hoop, meeting and parting, and it's like jazz, like a beautiful race, Ellen holding all these gazes and laughing out from the centre of it.

After a minute Sandra comes inside and walks up the stairs. Martin turns back to the newspaper. Over the ticking of the clock minutes later they can still hear Ellen breathing and giggling outside, and then finally the clack of the hoop falling to the cement.

In the afternoon Jocelyn picks it up and leaves it leaning against the wall, where one day it will rot and speckle with mould.

That evening after Sandra has gone to bed, Ellen says, 'He did it in front of her once.'

They are drinking wine, the bottle is near empty. Jocelyn says nothing. The blue letters have stopped coming, or almost, arriving only sporadically now.

Ellen says, 'Usually he was fairly quiet about it, but this time she was in the room and he pushed me up against a door and held me there and slapped my face. Poor Sandra, she just screamed and screamed.'

She stares into the air in front of her, one hand stroking the wide curve of her stomach. Any doubt Jocelyn has had is stroked away with that protective movement of her sister's fingers. She cannot speak, and Ellen wipes her own eyes with a handkerchief. They are both in silent tears. Martin stays quiet.

Ellen never asks about Pittwater. Jocelyn has twice begun to tell her about it; about the green water, Lion Island, the shell bucket. Ellen listened lightly, nodding, concentrating on a knitting pattern. Jocelyn took a breath to tell about her imagined garden, about Martin's beautiful book. But Ellen's needles clicked, and she lifted her head again and smiled. It was as though Jocelyn had been speaking of a day trip to the zoo.

'It sounds lovely.' *But you're home now.*

Jocelyn sometimes has the urge to write to Thomas. He and Jocelyn used to smile at each other when Ellen was being difficult, and Thomas would wink. Martin has convinced her not to, but she imagines long, hate-filled letters. She wants to write, Why did you do this? *To all of us.*

Martin has not been able to come for two weeks. There's a mountains cold snap, and the sky is grey almost every day. They order firewood. It has been a fortnight of wet kindling and doors banging through the house.

Jocelyn chops wood to warm herself up, and imagines returning to Pittwater: Sandra is settling in to the school. Ellen can look after herself . . . Jocelyn could surely leave them both here, step off the ferry on to the little wooden jetty and she and Martin could sit on the verandah, begin again.

It was winter when she was in England last, and she and Thomas had smoked marijuana after Ellen went to bed, silent, shutting doors firmly behind her. Thomas had started giggling like a child, sitting cross-legged in his socks among the cushions of the couch, and Jocelyn couldn't stop herself from giggling too. And she had felt sorry for him, married to Ellen. When they had finished the port and she blundered to her room that night she heard Ellen shouting on the floor above, and Thomas murmuring, and she had thought, *Poor Thomas.*

But Thomas has held her sister against a door, his hands at her throat.

She brings down the axe, and a sharp piece of wood goes spinning. She will not yet go back to Pittwater. She will stay, and in the autumn the baby will come and she will hold it in her arms and put her lips to its smooth, cool cheek. The baby will wake in the early dawn and silently watch the pale ceiling, its new Australian sky.

Ten

A T ONE END of their street a scrap-metal yard gives way to an abandoned collection of bronze garden statuary. Behind the fence wire, as Jocelyn walks with Sandra to school, the statues stare out. Closest is a woman, standing, her feet curled over the peak of a craggy mountain so that she looks down from a distance of almost twice the height of Jocelyn and Sandra below. The woman's arms are extended in a beckoning gesture, and her calf-length hair snakes down over two servant boys who crouch at her feet, gazing upwards. Their delicate toes hold the whole edifice off the ground. Their biceps curve under its weight, their thighs strain beneath the planes of their loincloths. One of the young men's hands rests over his colleague's lower back and he glances at him sideways.

When they first began taking this route to school Jocelyn would tell Sandra about when she and Ellen were small and would play among the statues. How they each claimed their own, visiting their giant iron dolls on the way to school, just like this. Ellen had the mermaids and goddesses, leaving the animals to Jocelyn.

Now, after the first week, Jocelyn's stories have run out. The iron goddess gazes out from behind the wire, ignoring the ambiguous longings of the servant boys, as Jocelyn and Sandra pass. Jocelyn is brisk but Sandra wanders slowly behind her, bobbing with each step so as to keep up the rhythmic bumping of her school case against her leg. A pile of rabbit traps rusts in the dirt.

They pass a garden fountain. Circling its shallow, waist-high bowl is a languid bronze mermaid, arms stretched in a backward dive, hair and tail meeting in a sensual flicker. A magpie scuffling in the dirt cocks its head, one-eyeing them as they pass. Then it lets out an arc of morning sound, those gulped, airy notes. They walk, the magpie goes back to scrabbling. Sandra holds out the palm of one hand and runs it along each diamond hole of the wire fence. When she gets rust on her fingers she wipes it on the skirt of her school uniform.

'Don't do that, sweetheart,' says Jocelyn, thinking about the waiting manuscript laid out on the glasshouse trestle table.

Past the clusters of stream-haired nymphs and one Queen Victoria, squatting in the dirt without her pedestal, the fence falls away and the motley collection of wild animals begins. Sandra leaves the path, goes to wander through the accidental animal park.

Jocelyn slumps. 'We haven't got time this morning, Sandra,' she lies. Trying to force a firm kindness into her voice, clinging to her need to remain serene, the unflappable aunt.

Sandra ignores her. The animals stare this way or that into the air. Three lions, manes streaming, face the narrow road, each with one giant paw extended towards the agricultural-pump workshop across the street. Jocelyn follows her, trying to stay calm. *The mother can shout, but the aunt stays calm.* The child will love the mother through the heart of her rage, but the aunt must stay calm or be cast adrift.

Four pelicans of varying sizes are pencilled in the space. Sandra moves through them to the life-sized bronze rhinoceros, its hide pimpled and ridged. It is her favourite.

'Come on, Sandra, we'll be late for school . . .'

Sandra watches Jocelyn while she drops the school case in the dust.

A fury rises up in Jocelyn. 'That's enough.' She meets Sandra's glare.

But Sandra keeps her eyes on her aunt's while she sits down, spreading the skirt of her uniform about her in the dust. The uniform Jocelyn washed at midnight and ironed at six so she had time to get Sandra up and washed and breakfasted and make sure Ellen could sleep in.

'*Sandra!*' And she finds herself with arms folded like any small-town mother, her voice shrill, fury rising, slipping into the territory where she might begin to cry with rage.

Don't take it personally.

Sandra, blank-faced, watches her, waiting for an explosion. She wriggles harder into the dirt. Jocelyn's throat is hurting with the effort of not crying. She can't speak.

She's a child.

Jocelyn doesn't believe it. She wants, more than anything, to march over and yank this child up by the arm and smack her legs hard, and even realising this does not stop the fact that she wants to hurt her. Not scare her, hurt her. Thomas comes into her mind. She feels sick.

She turns towards the road and watches the school bus pass, shiny little heads blobbed at its windows. The dust from the road and the vehicle exhaust settle over them as the bus heaves away. She waits, breathes deeply.

Its massive head down, its horn almost the size of Sandra as she leans into the protective bow of its knee, the rhinoceros stares beyond them both into the silvery mist and the eucalypts.

When Jocelyn returns to the house later, red-faced and near tears, Ellen laughs.

'You should have seen her getting on the plane at Heathrow.'

Jocelyn clatters dishes, tries to make herself calm. 'She hates me,' she says into the dishwater.

Ellen barks a laugh through a mouthful of toast, still leaning over a magazine. 'I know. She hates me too.'

Jocelyn rubs cereal from a dish in the water, shaking her head.

Ellen gets up from the table and comes to stand behind Jocelyn, puts her chin into the curve of her sister's neck. 'She's just being a little brat. But we are grateful,' Ellen says.

Jocelyn turns to apologise, and starts crying into Ellen's shoulder.

The currawongs start up outside.

When Martin arrives for the weekend they sit long at the table after dinner. Suddenly Ellen leans towards him, stabbing the air with her cigarette.

'Have you ever been unfaithful?' Her earrings swing and glint.

Martin blanches, snorts. 'Ellen! What a question!'

Ellen sees Jocelyn's face, and laughs. 'Not to *Joss*, of course, but before, I mean?'

'Ellen,' says Jocelyn. She is realising how much Ellen has drunk.

Martin blushes, silent now. Drinks from his glass.

'I think you've had too much wine,' Jocelyn says to Ellen, hears her own prudish voice.

Ellen ignores her. 'Oh come on, it's a fair question.' She leans to Martin again, grinning. Her neck is pale in the candlelight. 'You tell me and I'll tell you my secrets. We're almost family, aren't we?'

She swings again to look at Jocelyn. She seems very drunk now, leaning backwards in her chair, leering. Then says to her sister, a hardness edging beneath the question, 'Don't you *want* to know?'

Jocelyn stares back, feels her face grow hot. She and Martin don't look at each other. She stands to collect the dinner plates, hating her own primness. 'No,' she says quietly.

Ellen bursts out laughing, crows, 'Well, *that's* interesting!'

As Jocelyn leaves the room she hears Ellen say conspiratorially to Martin, 'I have. With a German.'

Later, as Jocelyn's undressing for bed, Martin comes into her room. 'Are you all right?' He puts his arms around her.

'I'm sorry,' Jocelyn says.

He laughs softly. 'I don't care. She was just pretty drunk, I suppose.'

He holds her in the hug, kisses her shoulder next to the strap of her slip.

After he has gone to his own room she lies in the dark, thinking of Ellen and a German and Thomas. And trying not to think about what Martin's expression might have been when she did not look at him across the table. Trying not to wonder why he had not said, *Of course not.*

Martin drives the road back to the city in the dark before dawn. Shivering to keep himself awake, trying to warm up, he flexes the muscles of his thighs repeatedly, shrugs his shoulders. He is glad this morning to be driving away from that house, from Ellen's voice. Rags of mist appear white on the road and sweep up suddenly above the car as he drives. He winds down the window and the icy air rushes in. He can make out the long hump of the mountain range now against the paler dark of the sky.

He is so tired. He slows the car, pulls over onto the gravel at the side of the road, and gets out, trudges to where the gravel meets the trees.

He stands there in the quiet, with his hands in his pockets, thinking of Jocelyn looking like a small girl when her sister talks. Thinking of Ellen's sly voice, her traps. The day to come at the surgery will be long, with all its complaints and smells, and there seems to be so much driving, all the bloody driving.

The sky is lightening, and he can smell the eucalypts. A bird whirrs. The mist still hangs in the air. If he wanted to, he could step slowly down into the dim fog and the dripping trees, and disappear into the bush.

In the weeks before Christmas the weather warms again and Jocelyn takes Sandra to the town swimming pool. She is going to teach her to swim. Sandra has been excited about coming, but the first day they arrive she is too embarrassed to change in the sunlit chlorine-scented rooms, and only after changing in a toilet cubicle will she walk to the pool, holding Jocelyn's hand. She stands at the edge, watching the other children leaping around in the water. She stands with her hands clasped in front of her thighs, arms stretched, covering her pudgy belly. The bright fibreglass panels of the fence cast a blue glow over her.

Jocelyn slips into the water first, the cold stunning her a moment, then lies on her back, trying to coax Sandra in. But Sandra will only sit on the edge with her legs dangling, ankles and feet moving from side to side in the water.

'You'll like it, I promise,' Jocelyn says, praying this to be true. At seven, she herself had taken almost a whole summer to put her head under. She remembers the slow, obstinate fear growing during the walk to every lesson;

the determination that today she would do it – but once in the water, thrashed by the kicks and splashes of other children, she'd lose her nerve, rearing up at the last second, breathless and petrified.

Martin and Ellen had argued about throwing a child in at the deep end. Each remembered the shock of it themselves, the shooting panic and splutter, the terrified disbelief at their parents' betrayal.

'But it was good for me,' Ellen said. 'You would never have got me in the water at all otherwise.'

Now Jocelyn and Sandra eye one another across the water, waiting it out. Sandra's small mouth is set hard, her arms folded with her hands tucked into her armpits. Jocelyn coaxes, jokes. Then flicks water, hoping Sandra will take up the game and kick a splash back at her. But Sandra only flinches and holds herself taut when Jocelyn reaches out a wet hand to her.

After twenty minutes of sitting in the shallow water watching toddlers with plastic toys and kickboards, Jocelyn water-crawls over to Sandra at the edge. 'It's all right, I won't make you. Just stay there and watch the other children while I do some laps in the big pool, okay?'

Sandra nods stiffly.

After swimming a lap Jocelyn lifts herself to hug the tiled edge, looking back at the children's pool, hoping to see Sandra wading or playing with the other children. But she is still there in the same spot, sitting in the blasting sun with her feet in the water.

Jocelyn sinks down in the water again, pushes off from the wall, stroking and breathing, emerging and submerging, concentrating on controlling her breath. She can't remove the image from her mind, of Sandra's expression when she had reached out from the water. She had seen in Sandra's face a kind of fear that children should not have.

On the way home in the car, Sandra says, 'You're my mum's sister.'

'Yes,' Jocelyn says.

'I'm going to have a sister,' Sandra says, lifting her chin. 'When I can swim, I'll teach her.'

Jocelyn nods as she drives, thinking of Ellen's baby. For whom they all wait, for whom they wish good things. The baby will have pianist's fingers, her grandfather's mouth. The baby will be an early walker, will be held in the water with her sister kissing her tummy.

On the next swimming outing Sandra sits again on the edge of the children's pool while Jocelyn swims laps. Then Jocelyn returns to the little pool and lies back in the shallow blue water at Sandra's feet, propped on her elbows, asking her about school, about the numbers she's learned, her friends. Sandra grips the concrete edge, dark hair hanging round her face. She sways her feet, answering yes and no, staring into the milky water. Then she says, 'My dad's not bad, you know.'

Jocelyn stops still in the water. 'I know,' she says quietly.

Sandra stares back, her dark eyes wide. 'Not on purpose.'

Jocelyn cannot say anything, only nods. They both turn to watch a boy walking with his father over the lawns towards the car park.

The heat intensifies, and Christmas is almost here. They have Sandra making decorations from cotton reels and milk-bottle tops, covering the dining table with glue and crêpe paper and tinsel. On the previous weekend Martin dragged in a tree and it leans in a corner of the living room, its tip curled against the ceiling.

Ellen and Jocelyn and Sandra take the train to Sydney and meet Martin for lunch, and then they all scatter through the department stores. In David Jones the pianist trills Christmas carols, and women strut, hats bobbing. Jocelyn chooses for Ellen an opal brooch, heavy and trimmed with gold lace, but it still has the feel of a stone taken from the earth. Only later does she realise she has wanted to give Ellen something from Australia. As if she is only a visitor.

Sandra's gifts are easy, and she piles them in her arms. A swimming costume with vertical red and white stripes, a box of pencils, books.

The four of them meet again at the department-store coffee lounge for afternoon tea, squirming to peek into one another's shopping bags. Martin is especially dramatic, snatching bags from Sandra's sight, making her shriek, and Ellen tells them both to be quiet. When Ellen turns away Martin makes a face and Sandra convulses with giggles. He murmurs to her, begging her not to tell, and they spend the hour whispering and sniggering.

Before bed on Christmas Eve, Jocelyn watches from the corridor as Ellen lowers a lumpy pillow-slip onto Sandra's bed. The child is heavily asleep on her back, one leg dangling from the bed and the sheet twisted across her, arms flung back.

At dawn Jocelyn wakes with Sandra's breath on her face, whispering loudly: '*I got Ludo!*' Holding up the box in the pale light. 'Do you want to play?'

Jocelyn, still half-asleep, shakes her head but moves over to let Sandra climb into her bed, and lies back with an arm around her. Sandra's halting, whispered reading of the game's instructions lullaby her back to sleep.

When she wakes later she has the bed to herself again, and she can hear Sandra's and Martin's shouts in the midst of the game downstairs.

Over tea and marmalade on the living-room floor they unwrap the presents, Jocelyn and Ellen still in their dressing gowns. It is Sandra's job to hand out the gifts, which she does solemnly, concentrating, only screeching when Martin takes his present from her politely and then, in contrast to the sisters who have been folding the discarded wrappings carefully, rips at his Christmas paper with a huge sweep of his arm.

The present is from Jocelyn. It is a framed pastel drawing of Pittwater. The headlands and bays are geometric blocks of colour, curving in blackened greens to the grey-blue sea. She had kept it on her dressing table for a week after she bought it, staring into it each morning and night. Inside the cool, layered colours is their abandoned summer by the water. She had left it there until the last possible minute before wrapping it.

Now Martin holds the drawing up, not speaking. On the back she has written: *For Martin, Christmas 1963. With all my love.*

His eyes shine, he wipes them with his fingers. He steps across the carpet and kisses her, and sits on the arm of the couch, his hand on her shoulder. He props the picture against the bookshelf, and keeps turning his head to look at it through the morning.

Then Ellen and Jocelyn begin the cooking. Blowflies knock lazily against the kitchen window, and the garden beyond is bleached white with heat and lack of rain. The temperature in the kitchen rises, and steam mists the windows.

After lunch Ellen takes Sandra with her for a sleep, and Martin and Jocelyn wash the dishes in the haze of the kitchen heat and lunchtime wine. He stands close to her, says, 'I love my present.' She turns to him, puts her arms around his neck. Then, hearing Ellen's voice in the hallway, they separate.

Jocelyn opens the door –

And finds Ellen sitting with the telephone in her hand, biting her lip, nodding, tilting a smile into the receiver while she listens to Thomas's voice from across the continents.

When Ellen finally comes into the living room and sees Jocelyn she says coolly that she booked the trunk call weeks ago. She adds, tapping a cigarette end on the packet in her hand, 'It's all right, I'll pay for it.'

Then Jocelyn's rage, grabbing Ellen by the shoulders,

shouting *Why?*, calling her *stupid*, shouting, *Have you ever thought* – and Martin calling after her to *calm down*.

Ellen puts out her own hands and elegantly removes Jocelyn's from her shoulders.

'It's Christmas. He has a right to know about his baby,' she says, cold-faced and tearless. Jocelyn stares at her, and has the blank realisation that she is outclassed, that Ellen is an old hand in the face of rage. And in the art of deception, writing back to Thomas on blue airmail paper all this time.

Eleven

I N THE FOLLOWING days, when Martin has gone back to the city, silence fills the house.

There is a rat in the kitchen, or rats. Jocelyn rummages through low cupboards in the laundry for traps, shuddering. She couldn't tell Ellen that when she reached into the fruit bowl on the sideboard this morning her hand landed on a half-eaten peach. She saw the combed tooth marks as she tossed it into the rubbish, and then quickly brushed the rat's droppings away as Ellen came in with the newspaper and took a peach in passing. And now, because Jocelyn let her eat the peach, she cannot tell her about the rat.

The only sound in the house is Sandra, shouting somewhere upstairs, with Ellen's voice a quiet, firm murmur against her yells. Ellen's self-control sends a surge of anger through Jocelyn.

She finds two greasy, fluffed traps at the back of a cupboard and drops them into the sink. Their size alone disgusts her. She pours boiling water over them to dislodge the fluff and wash from them the other nameless grease she doesn't want to think about, not caring at the foolishness of washing a rat trap before setting it.

Sandra has stopped shouting and slams a door. Jocelyn remembers it from childhood, her own hysteria and Ellen's smiling silence, the raised eyebrow, her folded arms.

She lifts the traps out by their corners with fingers and thumb and leaves them on the windowsill. Let Ellen see them, let her know she's shared a peach with a rodent's claws.

They haven't spoken again about the phone call to Thomas. Jocelyn hates Ellen for speaking to him, hates her own revived suspicion. She listens to Sandra still throwing things against a door, and tries not to think about Ellen and provocation and violence.

It's not her fault, thinking of Thomas and his hands, and Ellen's cool, cool face, watching him explode. *It's not her fault*. But the alternative edges at her.

The wireless in the living room is talking of the yacht race, which began three days ago in the sunlight ricocheting off Sydney Harbour. Now the rescue crews are leaving and returning to the Eden wharf, and the bodies of at least seven men are brought back, four boats still lost. She imagines those walls of sea curving over a tiny upturned white hull. What impulse is it that makes us throw ourselves into the sea?

It takes a week of baits and traps to catch the rat. Ellen has been oblivious, the whole time, of its scrabbling behind the kitchen dresser, and once Jocelyn saw it flashing through the crockery, its soft body elongating and yielding to the curves of the soup bowls. She had washed the entire cupboard's contents in boiling water that night after Ellen had gone to bed, then dried and replaced everything. Knowing as she climbed the stairs that the animal was probably already skittering through the shelves again.

One Sunday night Jocelyn thinks she hears Martin saying to her, almost inaudible in the dark, 'It will be all right.' She thinks he has whispered it, and listens hard, in the silence, to his breath. If he has said it she wants to believe it, to step away from this nameless fear she has been treading down daily.

In the morning she comes down to find the stiffened body of the rat in the trap, its head squashed awkwardly beneath the wire, and the base sticky with blood. Then she hears Ellen's bedroom door open above her and she bolts outside with it. Its glazed eye catches hers as she hurls it, still in the trap, behind the woodshed. She hurries back to clean the dark smudge from the linoleum with bleach before the others come down for breakfast.

When Martin comes in, scratching his cheek, sleepy and silent at the table beneath Sandra's chatter as he drinks his tea, Jocelyn watches him and wonders if he did whisper in the night. Sometimes these days it is difficult to recognise him.

School begins again, and when they resume their walks past the scrap yard a bronze crocodile has joined the animals. Sandra runs her fingers along its ridged skin. She seems to like going to school now, and talks about new friends, Elizabeth and Janet, who live in modern houses.

One day she says at home, 'Elizabeth hit me with a stick.' She lifts her skirt to show her thigh where a large red welt, a day later, is just subsiding.

'Never mind,' says Ellen, and pats her skirt down again. 'If it happens again you can tell the teacher.'

Once Sandra is in bed Jocelyn asks, 'Why don't you do anything about her being hit?'

Ellen laughs. 'Heavens, Joss, it wasn't like that.' She lifts her head to meet Jocelyn's eyes. 'They're just children. She's fine.' She takes a sip of water, waiting.

'No. She's not,' says Jocelyn, thinking of Ellen standing in a bedroom, waiting again for Thomas's raised hand to fall.

Alf shifts and yawns under the table. Jocelyn says, 'She needs to learn to stand *up* for herself. She needs to learn that if someone hits you, you don't just *take* it and wait for the next time. Or the next time or the next time.'

She hears the tremor in her own voice, her face is hot. She sees Ellen's open mouth, her shocked eyes. And still she gets up from her chair and leaves the room, leaving her sister sitting at the dining-room table, alone with those unsaid words. *You deserved it.*

After that night Jocelyn spends more and more time in the glasshouse working on the manuscript. The galleys keep arriving in the post; she has begun volume eight. She gets into the glasshouse early, opening the doors and windows to let out the heat that has already risen. Martin has begun to stay in Pittwater some weekends. Ellen annoys him more and more, Jocelyn knows.

As Ellen's belly grows larger her voice grows louder, she complains of an aching back, indigestion, headaches, she can't lift things, she's tired all the time. Wants Martin to check the baby's heartbeat constantly.

But Martin and Jocelyn do not talk about his staying away; it is a dangerous conversation they cannot have, they each know that Ellen's duplicity is the cliff over which they both might go hurtling.

In the glasshouse Jocelyn wills the pregnancy on, promises kindness towards Ellen. The baby will have brown eyes and lots of hair.

Flowers Rich and Strange.

The manuscript seems never-ending. She drags herself back to it; it's difficult to believe the contract will finally finish in a few months, a few more volumes.

The flora of Australia, often oddly named, reflect the harsh diversity of the continent. While much of the country might be described as drab, some of its wild flowers are shockingly brightly coloured. Consider the Sturt Desert Pea – low-growing, bright red and large-petalled, with one bulbous black eye – that bursts into bloom from seed after desert rains.

The tone of the manuscript irritates her now, with its constant exclamations about the strangeness of Australia. In it she hears the voices of Ellen's London girlfriends, sees their flashed up-and-down glances at her own clothes, hears the unspoken word, 'colonial'.

In a corner of the glasshouse, under a pile of books at the far end of the trestle, are her drawings, the notes she made at Pittwater, the collected specimens, the coloured swatches. And the beautiful book. She remembers that evening now as if it were a decade ago, the night she told Martin about her garden and felt something inside herself spark.

She turns back to the manuscript, leaving the garden to lie where it is, buried beneath the weight of her days.

On the next trip to the swimming pool Sandra lowers herself into the water.

Every week until now she has sat on the edge, feet in the water, refusing to get in. Jocelyn chats into Sandra's silence, about the coming baby, about school. Summer is nearing an end and the pool is quieter; only two mothers with children play in the other end, splashing and squawking.

Jocelyn lies on her back in the water with her eyes closed, the sun warm on her face and neck. Then, beneath the splashes and shrieks of the other children, she hears a low plonking. She opens her eyes to see Sandra standing in the water, waist deep, arms out from her sides, taking small gasping breaths.

Staring across the liquid surface to the tiled opposite wall, shivering, her face terrified and determined, Sandra begins to walk on the slick floor towards the steps at the end. The water deepens, rises higher up her stomach, her chest. She still holds her arms high out of the water.

Jocelyn sits, not moving. She wants to glide over, to guide her, but stays where she is, holding her breath. Then Sandra reaches the steps and hauls herself out to stand shivering on the edge. Jocelyn wants to jump up and scream, but doesn't want to turn the heads of the other swimmers. Instead she wades through the shallows to the edge where Sandra stands, and she sinks to her knees in the water, planting three flourishing kisses on the toes of her niece standing, dripping and grinning down at her, on the tiles.

Twelve

ELLEN'S BELLY CURVES outwards now and Jocelyn begins to rest her own hand over it when she is near her. From talk of the baby has emerged a kind of peace between them, and when they stand in the small kitchen facing one another it is as though the child belongs to both of them, is growing between them.

They do not mention Thomas; they still have not spoken of him since Christmas Day, and somehow Jocelyn tells herself Ellen has stopped writing to him. But as the birth of his child draws near, his presence here is as taut as a trip-wire.

Sandra now leans into Jocelyn when she is near. When Sandra sits in her lap to be read to, Jocelyn rests her cheek on her niece's head, turns herself concave to accommodate her, to draw closer around her skinny angles and soft skin.

The swimming lessons have taken on a zealous air since the day Sandra got into the water. They both run out of the house on swimming day now, clutching towels, racing each other to the car. At the pool Sandra jumps in, still straining to keep her head out of the water, but allowing herself to begin to enjoy the splash and chaos.

Then one day she puts her head under and comes up spluttering, hair streaming and eyelashes dripping, clutching Jocelyn's arm under the water. Jocelyn screams, dives down to lift Sandra shrieking from the water, and they fall back in together laughing, Sandra's arms and legs wrapped around Jocelyn. The small, cold, wet face next to her aunt's, the little limbs hard and angular, and Jocelyn thinks, *This is how you love a child.*

Afterwards they sit on the hot cement eating ice-blocks, and Jocelyn says, 'Did you know you're a brave, strong girl?'

Sandra, sitting in the bright nest of her blue towel, holds the red ice-block sideways, dips her head to suck it, her damp hair in scraggly tails. She lifts her face, meets Jocelyn's eyes. 'Yes,' she grins. 'I knew.'

The three of them spend hours choosing baby names. Sandra has a long list, either flamboyant or dull, all traceable to some particular place in her small world.

Alf, Elizabeth, Marion Barrow from the author's name on the cover of one of her books, with its pictures of fairies and English wood-nymphs. 'Thomas,' she says once. Ellen and Jocelyn avoid each other's glances over her head.

Ellen reads biblical names out loud from lists in books. Ezekiel! Isaiah! – they laugh. It is March, summer is at an end. Ellen's skin is ripe-looking, luminous. She sways as she walks.

Every day now when she finishes her afternoon's work Jocelyn goes into the baby's room they have made in the old sewing room at the end of the hall. A tiny cupboard of a room, but big enough for the narrow cradle their father had made from kitchen chairs, for Ellen, and then Jocelyn, as babies. And a small chest of drawers. Jocelyn has painted them white, painted the walls of the room as well. She leaves the window open so the paint smell will be gone by the time the baby comes.

Sometimes Ellen dozes on the couch in the living room in the afternoons. Often, as she lies there she will lift her blouse, rest with her arms clasped behind her head on a cushion, and then she and Jocelyn and Sandra will wait, watching her skin for the subterranean movement. The first time they saw it they gasped; these days they give small cheers, calling *Hello baby*, calling welcome to the shape shifting and sliding beneath Ellen's skin.

The baby is due in six weeks. Martin examines Ellen, talking to her in George's surgery. Jocelyn sits in the waiting room, hears them murmuring from behind the door. It is strange, this intimacy they have without her.

The house grows quieter, and Ellen's moodiness returns. She snaps at Sandra. Martin and Jocelyn walk quietly about the house. It is as though they are all animals, crouching, bristling, waiting for birth.

On the Nullarbor Plain, stretching across two states, is the longest stretch of straight road in the world. The ninety-mile straight is part of the traveller's journey across the Great Australian Bight, where the desert falls into the sea.

The aerial photographs show it: the flat, scrubby edge of the continent broken off like a biscuit, sheer cliff walls plunging hundreds of feet into the ocean. On those high desert plains, once a sea bed, the earth is apparently scattered with tiny white shells. Another photograph shows a tourist standing suicidally close to the edge, his feet on the crumbling earth, behind him only sea and sky.

Jocelyn puts down the manuscript and picks up the newspaper. It is Sunday, and Martin has left a day early, his car pulling out of the driveway after lunch.

The newspaper headlines are full of a young school teacher gouged by a shark, sitting on his surfboard in the lulling water off a South Australian beach in the falling evening. From his hospital bed, where his thigh has taken eighty-seven stitches, he tells reporters about his panic, about the miraculous wave, the big, beautiful wave that took his broken board and him, blood-visioned, 'right to the sand'. He tells how he lay on his back in the foaming sand, holding the pages of his wound together with both his hands, watching the blood and waiting to die.

It is the seventh reported shark attack in the country this summer: two in New South Wales, three in South Australia, one each in Western Australia and Victoria. People talk about the sharks over their dinner tables, slapping mosquitoes from their legs. They talk about the warmth of the water this year, and all the other theories as to why the sharks are coming so close to the edges of the land. They enjoy their growing knowledge of the names of the different species, they imagine each swimmer, fisherman, surfer. Shuddering, they say *Poor bastard*; they think of the last sight of your life being a brackish shadow and then not knowing water from pain or air. The newspapers gabble over it, *The season of the sharks*, feasting on it, revisiting every attack since 1934 with each new report.

Sandra has been whining all weekend, following Ellen around. She wanted something to eat, she was bored, she had nobody to play with, she wanted to take her shoes off. With each wail Ellen grew cooler and harder, responding to her daughter less and less. Yesterday Jocelyn had tried to intervene, offering to read a story, or take her for a walk, but Sandra only stared at her for a second, and moaned, 'I don't want *you.*' Then trailed off after her mother again. Ellen sat down in the living room and tried to read the paper under the nag of Sandra's voice, smoking a cigarette, now and again silently twisting her arm from under Sandra's clasping little hands. After a long silence beneath Sandra's whines and wails, Ellen turned and clawed her daughter's fingers from the arm of her chair. She neared her face to Sandra's suddenly alarmed one and shouted at her:

'*Get* out of my sight, to your room, you little shit. *Go on! Go to your room.*'

Sandra's face crumpled, she let out another melodramatic moan, sobbing, '*But I* WANT *you!*' and then gasped, hysterical, as Ellen leaned out of her chair with a raised hand and lunged at her. She stumbled, howling, out the door.

Martin had shifted in his seat at the dining table, folded his arms again over the Saturday paper. Jocelyn put down her coffee cup. Ellen had grinned tightly at them from her chair.

'Just another afternoon in motherhood's paradise, darlings.' Lit another cigarette, inhaled deeply as she began again to read.

From upstairs came the sound of Sandra's fury, of a door repeatedly slammed, her screams echoing through the house and across the garden. Martin got up from the table.

Minutes later Jocelyn found him in his room, pushing his clothes into a bag.

'You're not leaving.' Trying to force kindness into her voice.

'I have to get some stuff ready before Monday.'

Her goodwill deserting, she flared. 'For God's sake, Martin, she's just a child. That's what children do. You just have to ignore it.'

He stood up suddenly. 'It's not Sandra, Joss. It's Ellen. Why doesn't she bloody well *do* something?' He jammed the clothes in harder.

Jocelyn took a breath to defend her sister – the childhood reflex.

Martin said, holding her hands, 'I know, I'm sorry. It's just today, I can't stand it. Next weekend will be better.'

In the driveway they kissed through the window of the car before he drove off. This time Jocelyn did not fight the imprisoned feeling: she may as well have manacles on her wrists.

When she came inside and stood with her arms folded in the living room, Ellen said lightly, without looking up, 'What's Martin's problem?'

Jocelyn stared at her, shaking her head. 'He can't stand being around you two fighting.'

Ellen kept reading, said, 'Oh, for Christ's sake.'

Jocelyn walked from the room, slamming the door behind her. She stalked into the glasshouse, slamming that door so hard one of the glass panes cracked. Not noticing Sandra watching her from her bedroom window.

Later in the silent evening Sandra creeps down from her room. Jocelyn walks past the living room to see Sandra on her mother's knee, Ellen with her arm around her, murmuring into her hair.

Something about this conciliation makes Jocelyn's own rage rise up again. For they have each other, through their moods and tantrums, and Jocelyn is only the aunt, with their meals to cook and their clothes to wash, and Martin driving as far away from her as he can.

On Tuesday Ellen says, 'I feel so tired. I can't bear the idea of another month of this.' She looks pale.

Good, thinks Jocelyn. They have hardly spoken since the weekend, except in terse, necessary phrases over meals or housework.

Ellen says, 'Is Martin coming on the weekend?'

'I don't know.' Jocelyn does not look at her sister.

Martin telephones on Thursday. 'Let's go away for a few days. I can take until Wednesday,' he says. His voice is excited. 'I've thought out the route, we'll go west, camp along the way.'

Jocelyn holds the receiver in her hand in the dark hallway. She thinks of a grey road and the pale country opening up around them, a fire at night.

'Ellen won't like it.'

Martin groans. 'Jesus, she'll be fine.'

'I know, but I haven't been very nice.'

'Look, I'll talk to her. We'll leave early Saturday. She'll be fine.'

Jocelyn returns to the living room, says to Ellen, 'Martin and I are going away for a few days, camping.'

Ellen looks up suddenly. Her hand comes instantly, protectively, over her belly.

Jocelyn says, 'It's only for a few days, Ellen.'

Ellen first says nothing; then, very quietly, 'Do you have to go?'

Jocelyn closes her eyes. Guilt seeps in, she wavers. And then, remembering Ellen's dismissal of Martin on the weekend, she hardens.

'Yes. I think you're being a bit dramatic. It's only for a few days.'

Ellen says nothing, turns to stare into the fireplace.

Later Jocelyn lies in bed, reasoning with herself. Calls up images of Ellen's sarcasm, of Martin's car pulling away down the drive, pushes away the picture of Ellen's face by the fire this evening and how tired she looks. Thinks of Martin's skin, beneath the canvas of a tent, and the sound of trees moving through the night.

In Ellen's bedroom after a late dinner on Friday evening, Martin presses on her belly. The baby has turned around again, its head nestling under one side of her ribcage.

'Good as gold.' These silly phrases that come from his doctor's mouth.

Ellen sits up, pulls down her blouse. She yawns, it is eleven o'clock.

Outside in the driveway the car is packed with Martin's small tent and a few things; Jocelyn is washing dishes in the kitchen below them.

To Martin, Ellen looks utterly healthy; it is Jocelyn who has shadows under her eyes. 'You just need some more rest,' he says. He starts to put away the stethoscope, makes his movements brisk.

She nods, smiles an apology. 'I'm sorry I've made things difficult for you and Joss.'

He shakes his head, glances at her and then down at the bedspread, waves away her words.

She nods again. 'Thank you, Martin, I do appreciate everything you both are doing.'

He nods, says again, 'Get some rest.' A formality has fallen over them now. He puts a hand on her arm, tells her to go to bed.

It's dark in the morning when Jocelyn and Martin drink tea across the kitchen table from each other. The room is cold, there's fog outside, lit white by the moon.

Jocelyn smiles over her cup, whispers, 'It's like going on holidays when you're a kid.' He grins back in the gloom.

Some hours later the light pales as they drive through the first town, its clock and civic hall small but majestic in the rising morning.

Martin is singing 'Fly Me To The Moon' to her in a loud voice, his hands on the wheel.

She's smiling through the glass of her window over this small town, its dried-out golf course, its upright buildings.

She joins in. '*In other words, darling, kiss me . . .*'

The car enters a long ragged avenue of eucalypts, leaning high above the road, a canopy over Martin and Jocelyn and the Sinatra song below.

They drive west and the air warms, grows hot. On the second afternoon the car jostles over sandy soil beside a vast platinum lake. She watches a pelican in its long, low sweep from air into water, its landing, erect drifting. From the stippled sheet of water the trunks and broken branches of dead trees lift like flower heads, and everything has a sheen in this late afternoon sun.

They set up their camp by the lake. The heat is heavy, and now, out of the rushing air of the car, they are both sweating by the time they pitch the tent. The idea of a campfire is unbearable.

'I'm going for a swim,' she says, and after a minute he follows her, over the tussocky sand to the water's edge. They undress, hang their clothes on a dead limb. There is a tide-mark on the trees which, from a certain angle, accords exactly with the horizon behind. She walks into the cool water. Martin wades in behind her, they are silent with heat and tiredness from the long day's driving. The tree limbs are broken against the sky.

This flat silver water moves over her body like a blade, and she sinks slowly to her knees with the tight thread of the waterline moving across her skin. Martin floats on his back. For an instant she sees them, two naked and new-made beings, lying baptised in a silver garden.

And then the water ripples, the air cools.

'Thank God,' Martin moans, then upends ducklike, kicking a splash for the breeze. Jocelyn stands to cool herself in it, hand over her eye into the sun, water at her thighs.

'Do you think it's a storm?'

Martin looks. And it is true, a huge, dark wall of sharp-edged cloud to the north. He groans, 'That would be bloody right.'

The breeze is stronger, the water is gooseflesh now. They scurry back over the sand, clothes bunched in their

arms, he slaps her bottom and they screech as he scram-
bles to overtake her. The absurdity of a storm, biblical in
its sudden looming. And now it's a wind, not a breeze,
and they shimmy their wet bodies into the dry clothes
that stick to their skin.

The cloud breaks before they have a chance to eat, so
they shove things from the car inside the opening of the
tent, and clamber in to sit on their piled blankets with a
bottle of sherry and a lantern and an ashtray. They dig
channels with a spoon in the sand floor to direct the
rivulets of water away, and then perch on their blankets,
a packet of biscuits between them. As the rain beats down
through the night they get drunk, and became hysterical
when a little channel overflows or one of them touches
the canvas to send the water pouring in. Eventually one
or other of them dozes, the lamp still lit, clutching
suddenly at the noise of a thunderbolt and the snapping
and dripping of the canvas through the night.

In the morning the storm is gone and the sky is cloud-
less. Jocelyn leaves Martin snoring in the tent and walks
along the waterline, watches another pelican's wavering
landing.

She finds a few bits of miraculously dry kindling
beneath the truck and manages to light a fire for the billy.
Sits on an upturned bucket and closes her eyes, listening
to the quiet and the birds and the riffling water.

They travel many miles like this. On the last night, at the campfire, their conversation takes turns, resting and murmuring, and with a stick Jocelyn shifts and nudges at the small caves of light within the fire. They sit with one another beneath the trees in the ball of the night. The earth imperceptibly turns.

'Ah, Christ, tomorrow.' Martin sighs, reaches out a hand to receive hers and she sees his skin in the red fire-light, as though he is from another land. They are beautifully tired, have travelled so far just to sit here together on this sandy soil, this place where it is darkest and most alone.

She moves to lie against him, feeling his pulse through her own skin, and they watch the flames. Around them the high lacy walls of the bush, the trees' quiet shifts and cracks, the starred sky.

Thirteen

THE TOWN'S OUTSKIRTS come as a flat relief; the haggard bowling green, the new industrial buildings soft in the evening light. Both their backs ache, they have driven many hours today, eating sandwiches as they travelled, stopping only minutes for petrol.

Through the afternoon they have begun, separately, to think about the days to come; Ellen's moods, Sandra's tantrums. Jocelyn has been rehearsing in her head the guilty conversation, Ellen's taut face and curt replies. Jocelyn will cook them a nice dinner, will insist on Ellen's going early to bed, will play with Sandra, will let Ellen be right. Will finally finish the baby's room, smooth a white newborn's quilt over the cot. The baby will soon be here; it will have perfect lips and be rocked to sleep.

There are no lights on at the house when they drive in at a quarter to seven. At the front door Jocelyn takes down a note, written in a neighbour's hand.

Please come and collect Sandra.

Fourteen

I N THE HOSPITAL corridor the air goes meaty, whistles. Martin is not there behind his words. The baby. She is feeling the down of hair on her own face. Her brain coils, slithers. He is standing there like a piece of something. Glass? Her heart understands something, begins juddering in her chest. She tries to make him out, in the corridor, in a hospital.

Died. Is dead.

Breath comes in and goes out.

Her voice says, 'Where?' It is not her voice.

The piece of glass says, 'She's in there, I've told her.'

Hospital light greenish over them in the hallway. Martin is pointing an arm back at a door. He wants her to walk through it. She moves her legs.

He turns and walks down the corridor, away from her.

Through the door is a room with six beds, six women. Jocelyn has to look around for a minute before she finds Ellen, at the far end of the room. Outside the window glows the pale ball of a streetlight, as though this is any ordinary night.

Ellen is lying on her side, knees slightly bent, her hands together under her head in the way that Jocelyn has seen Sandra sleeping. Jocelyn wants to turn and walk out of the room, out of this building, out of the town into the bush, climb a tree, hide in a cave.

As she walks over she sees one of the other women is feeding her baby, its small head downy and snuffling at her breast. The woman cradles her child and looks carefully at her orange bedspread as Jocelyn passes.

She walks around to the chair beside Ellen's bed. Ellen is staring, eyes open and wet. Her face is grey, her hair damp. Jocelyn pulls out the chair and sits down.

'Where's Martin?' Ellen says. Jocelyn shrugs.

She puts her hand out and Ellen takes it, pulls it to her and holds it under her head between her own two hands.

Jocelyn remembers her childhood nightmares. *Think of something nice.*

The baby at the next bed starts to wail, its mother shushing and shushing it. A nurse comes and draws a curtain around Ellen's bed.

Jocelyn sits there in the chair with her fingers in Ellen's two praying hands under her face for a long time.

The next-door baby settles. Beyond the streetlight the moon comes up outside.

Fifteen

MARTIN IS STANDING hunched over the fire, head touching the mantelpiece and arms up like someone sleeping on a desk, when she comes in. He straightens slowly.

The air moves between them, into their separate bodies. Deathly as water.

'Where's Sandra?'

He points upwards to the bedroom, she nods.

The hallway beyond the dining room is piled with the mess of their trip: the tent-bag, the swag, their bag of dirty clothes. It seems something from her childhood, when they drove up to the house this evening, a memory of years ago, not hours.

He has a drink in his hand, pours her one. She takes it, seeing her own fingers move.

She sits down, watches the vaporous brandy, its slow gold wave.

'Did you talk to George?' she asks him. The air moves. He looks at her, her red eyes.

'Yes,' he says. 'He tried forceps, but it took too long. Died soon after he got him out. Just after seven. Just as I got to the delivery room.'

He doesn't say, *Just in time to take in this memory I will never lose, that wet weight in my hands.*

He pauses, says instead, 'George doesn't know what exactly happened. He's done it before . . .'

Martin is very small in this room with its rushing air. She knows his answer before she asks him, the coral rosettes of the carpet swell.

'But you know. If we were here, you could have done it,' she says. She knows it, but cannot stop the awful bloom of his one word:

'Yes.'

In the morning Jocelyn does not wake Sandra, but she comes into the kitchen anyway, hair unbrushed, and dressed for school. Jocelyn puts her arms around the girl. Sandra stays there, leaning against her body.

Jocelyn says, 'You don't have to go to school today, sweetheart. Do you understand what's happened?'

Sandra stares back, says, 'Yes. Is Mum in the hospital still?'

Jocelyn nods, stroking her niece's arm.

'I want to go to school then,' Sandra says.

They walk to the scrap yard, and Sandra moves to the crocodile, climbs and straddles its ridged back. Jocelyn follows, unsure of every movement.

She sits down behind Sandra, sideways on the crocodile's tail.

Sandra says, 'Where's the baby?'

Jocelyn breathes out. Takes another breath.

Then Sandra says, 'I know it's dead, but where is it?'

She turns and runs her finger over the bronze rises and dips of the crocodile's back, and Jocelyn touches her own finger to the small hollow in the nape of Sandra's neck. 'I don't know,' she says.

'Was it a sister?' says Sandra.

Jocelyn begins to cry.

Sixteen

THE FLYSCREEN DOOR bangs through the night. Somehow he has come back here, driven through the afternoon into the evening, finally parked at the roadside near the jetty. Slept in his car waiting for the first-light ferry, climbed aboard in his slept-in clothes, said hello to the captain. Walked the jetty after the boat had trundled back across that small body of water, come into his house and fallen onto the bed, slept through into that night and the next day.

He wakes like this three mornings in a row, blindly, as if drunk, knowing something terrible has happened. His blurred thoughts shift tectonically, the masses of his memory faltering, fault lines dividing. And then he is awake and he has always known this blood-red, rotting truth.

He walks to the kitchen. Pulling out a chair takes all his strength; it is the heaviest thing he has ever touched. He does not eat. Feels the acid of vomit jerk upwards through his oesophagus, charges across the room to lean exhausted and spitting quietly into the kitchen sink. Feels the decaying film of his blood.

There is only the webbed realisation. His thoughts spread in rivulets, but stop at the edge of it. Only the hospital, the green light of the corridor, a baby's feet, *Stop*.

Seventeen

ELLEN STAYS IN the hospital bed for a week, getting up only for the toilet. Nurses come and tidy up around her. After two days their movements are brisker when they draw back her curtain. Their voices are deliberately bright, and have grown louder, as though her time in bed has made her into a child.

'Perhaps they are right,' she tells Jocelyn, taking the magazine from her and putting it on the cabinet with the others. It is the *Australian Women's Weekly*. It has a photograph of the Queen on the front. She is pearly skinned; she has a crimson cloche hat and matching lips. Her hand is a white glove.

'They have told me to have another child.'

Jocelyn nods. 'They told me you should, too.'

'I didn't tell them about Thomas.'

'Me neither.'

They look at one another for a second, then at the things in the room. Green Jacquard bedspread with BLUE MOUNTAINS DISTRICT HOSPITAL printed down the middle of the bed. The bunch of late roses Jocelyn has brought, their bright heads too heavy for the stems. A few swollen rosehips.

'Where is Sandra?'

Every day she asks Jocelyn this.

'At school. She's all right. I took her there. I will pick her up this afternoon.'

Ellen nods, slowly. She has not asked about Martin since the first day.

'Do you know what I thought last night?' Ellen says. She's looking at Jocelyn with glassy eyes. She does look like a child, Jocelyn thinks, with her pale face and her hair brushed by someone else – a nurse?

'I was thinking about the babies at the end of the corridor.'

There is a room beyond the nursery, for the illegitimate children, waiting for the adoption people to collect them.

'I thought,' Ellen's eyes fill again, 'I thought, I could just go and pick up one of those babies out of his cot, and we could all go home.'

Jocelyn says nothing. Then, softly, 'Yes.'

From the hallway the crying of a baby is getting louder,

and they hear through the curtain a nurse's raised voice over the cries, bringing the baby in to its mother.

'Here you are, she's a greedy little thing,' the nurse calls over the shrieking breaths of the baby. The mother's voice says something, and then the baby's gasps stop suddenly, and there's a sucking noise.

Ellen's curtain rips open. The metal rings make a scraping sound along the bar. A nurse stands there with a thermometer, and Jocelyn has to make room for her to move over next to Ellen. The nurse says nothing while Ellen opens her mouth for the thermometer and lifts her wrist to have her pulse taken. The nurse presses her fingers over the veins in Ellen's wrist and cups in her other hand the small clock dangling from a chain at her breast. Ellen sits with her mouth pursed around the thermometer, staring at the cream-painted iron bar of the bedstead.

Jocelyn does not know how much longer she can stand to come here.

The nurse looks across at her, the sister. Says nothing, but moves to the bottom of the bed and writes something on a chart, then bustles past Jocelyn again to begin tidying the magazines and pushing the vase of flowers to the back of the cabinet. A rose softly collapses, scattering petals across the floor. The nurse sighs loudly and bends to gather them up. She looks at Jocelyn as she rises.

'Hello,' says Jocelyn evenly.

'She'll be going home tomorrow. She's perfectly all right,' the nurse says, and tosses the red petals into the paper bag taped to the side of Ellen's cabinet.

After she has gone Jocelyn stares into the bag, at the red glow of the petals against the white paper.

Ellen says, quietly, 'It seems you're to be punished as well.'

The next morning, as they leave the ward, a nurse hands Ellen an envelope. She does not open it until she is in the car, sitting beside Jocelyn while they ease backwards, out from the parking space. She reads the piece of paper, then folds it back into its envelope as they drive out along the town's streets with the autumn trees red against the sky, the closed fibro houses white behind their brick fences. 'It's a bill,' she says. She stares ahead at the road. 'For the burial.'

When they get home the red roses are bright against the house. Ellen, moving slowly, pushes past them into the hallway, walks up the stairs to her bedroom and shuts the door behind her.

Sandra is at school, Martin in Sydney. Jocelyn lights a match to the newspaper and kindling bundle in the living-room fireplace, but it won't catch. The air is damp, and the house is cold. When she thinks of Martin, she can only picture him as if in a reduced photograph, very small and far away. The damp newspaper curls at its cindered edge, but won't flame. Jocelyn stands up to go into the kitchen for drier paper, and to light the oven. But when she stands she is overcome by the weight of her own limbs, and she sits down in the old red armchair. Ellen's small overnight suitcase is by the living-room door. Jocelyn knows it is full of baby clothes.

Each day she wakes, afraid of the length of the day ahead. She sees it as a broad, greyish mass. Pushes it from her mind and focuses on the immediate tasks. Get up, get Sandra up, shower, make the coffee. Make the bed. She falls back to sleep and dreams of walking in a vast desert, there is an undertow of fear but all around her the pinks and blues and oranges of porous stone hold her vision. She is alone.

Sandra begins to wet the bed, so each morning Jocelyn's ritual now is to wake her, send her to her bath, and then bend and straighten over the bed, gathering up the damp sheets and Sandra's nightie, to carry them downstairs to the laundry. The nightie still faintly warm with the smell of her urine and her sleeping body.

Ellen wakes earlier than any of them, despite the sedatives. Jocelyn's other job is to go into her sister's room and draw her curtains. When she opens the door Ellen is always alert, her head still on her pillow, her expression taut for bad news. Jocelyn's unspoken duty is the ritual of letting her sister know with routine and silence that Sandra has not also died in the night. With the opening of the curtains, every morning Ellen's face relaxes back into emptiness, and she closes her eyes. They exchange no words until later in the morning.

When Martin comes up from the city Jocelyn watches him pull himself out of the car, and stand for a moment facing the garden. If someone else saw him they would think here was a man returning from the city, stepping into the cool release of his home. But she sees him from behind the window glass, delaying his walk up the drive, observes him wishing he could disappear, wishing he did not have to arrive at their front door. She feels it every day herself.

On this first evening she tries not to notice his slowness, tries to wind up some goodwill towards him, staying an instant longer when she kisses him.

They eat at the dining table with Ellen. Jocelyn heaves the conversation along, asks Martin about the drive here, about work, tells them about something funny Sandra said on a walk to school, asks Ellen about some memory when they were children. They answer in monosyllables, and shortly Jocelyn too falls silent, pushing the food across her plate.

After the dinner dishes are cleared Jocelyn makes her way through the garden to the glasshouse, sits and rolls a marijuana cigarette. Twenty minutes later, Martin opens the door. The glasshouse hangs with the drug's pungence.

The air tenses but nothing is said. He stands at the table next to her, looking over the encyclopaedia manuscript and its ragged edges, using his hand to wipe the dust from its pages. She leans back in her chair, puts a foot on the trestle and gently rocks the kitchen chair on its back legs while she takes her time unfolding the second tobacco paper, creasing it, sprinkling the leaf and tobacco shreds.

He walks along beside the table, finds her old garden drawings and scraps, pulls them out and leafs through them, slowly. She can think of absolutely nothing to say. She trills the rolled cigarette in her mouth, lights it, offers it to him. He walks out.

They spend these few evenings in separate misery. He does not go to Jocelyn's bed in the night, and he leaves before any of the others are awake.

Back at the Pittwater house he sits on the verandah, pushing his glass and ashtray from the previous week to the end of the table. He watches the waves and thinks of the tide, and wishes for something to save them all.

The Chinese man who gave Martin the mud crab does not have bronchitis. Months after that first visit he had returned to the surgery, thin and still coughing, and now cancer of the lung has been confirmed in a brief letter from the respiratory specialist.

In the surgery, Mr Ho had sat neatly on the chair, waiting. The surgery was hot, the whirring portable fan on the filing cabinet in the corner doing little to cool the room.

Martin spent half an hour with him, trying to explain, drawing pictures of his body. He drew the torso too large, the lungs wobbly, and afterwards the drawing was covered in small specks of pen where he had tried to explain the disease to the man.

'Sick, here. Very sick.'

'Ah,' Mr Ho said. He smiled politely. He coughed again, waiting.

'You need special medicine, from the hospital. To make you better. You need to go back to Doctor Bennett.'

Mr Ho understood 'hospital'. He smiled again, unhappily, and shook his head. 'No hospital.'

The room was unbearably hot. Martin stood and went to the door, called to Susan, asking for two glasses of water. He closed the door again. Mr Ho was sitting very straight in his chair. Martin cast around in his mind for a way to communicate.

He knew nothing of China. He had a friend who went to Bangkok once, on his way back from Europe. A man from the hotel hired a boat and they travelled for an hour along the coffee-brown river, beside the houses curving and tilting on their stilts. Most houses had at least one room collapsing into the water, Martin's friend had said, the floors curling down like paper. Martin has been to Chinatown in Sydney several times, has walked along the streets looking through the butchers' windows at the bright red carcasses dangling. None of this was useful here.

'Can you bring a friend who speaks English? Your daughter?' he asked. He was aware of his voice becoming louder.

'No,' said Mr Ho, politely.

Martin decided to try to find someone who spoke Chinese.

'Come back to see me in one week, all right? Yes? You come back on Monday? Bring your daughter?'

Mr Ho coughed, brightened. 'Yes! Goodbye, Doctor.' At the door he turned suddenly. 'You like crab?'

'Yes! Yes!' Martin had forgotten about the mud crab. 'Yes! Bad cook, but yes!'

They laughed and shook hands, and then Mr Ho walked away. He turned out through the glass door and stepped down, delicately, into the city.

Eighteen

WHEN SANDRA IS at school Jocelyn tries to work on the proofreading, that sprawling mess of words and pictures. It has become an anvil, its pile of manila folders always in the corner of her vision where she has carried it from room to room.

Alf twitches in his sleep on the couch, a charcoal map of the world on the soft pink skin of his belly. He has taken to scrabbling heavily up onto the furniture, and nobody stops him. In the grey light from the living-room window Jocelyn sees the slackness in his skin, his slow, heavy breath. He is the only sound sleeper in the house.

Once, in the kitchen, Ellen says quietly to the window over the sink, 'I wish I was dead.' At the table behind her, Sandra puts a piece of toast into her mouth and watches out at her mother's world, as if they are both trapped in an iron boat beneath the sea.

Jocelyn sits in George Blewitt's office. He has anatomical diagrams on the walls. The lungs, the spine, coloured pink and white. The doctor leans forward, writing on his prescription pad. The human hand has twenty-seven individual bones. He sits up then, and puts down his pen. He smells of breakfast foods when he talks to her, and she is nauseated. 'Now,' he says. Trying to be kind. 'How are you today.' It is not a question. He says it like a gentle sigh. He knows Martin has refused to treat any of them any longer.

She looks at him. She tries to be *kind* as well. She does not know what that word means; knows people want it but it has only the sound of teeth and mouths to her.

'How is your sister?' he says to the arm of her chair.

She can answer this. 'Terrible. Not sleeping. She hears cries now.'

George is upset. She knows she upsets him, is sorry in a way.

That first time, Ellen had sat up in bed when Jocelyn went in. 'I can't help it, Joss,' she'd said and looked down at the eiderdown. 'I've been hearing it cry all morning. I got out of bed, early. I thought it was coming from the *kitchen*.' She stared at her sister, glass-eyed, pale. 'I think I'm going mad.' She breathed the words out, pinching and unpinching the yellow flowers of the eiderdown between her fingers, staring up at Jocelyn. Who only moved her head, slowly, who could not say anything.

Who cannot say anything now to the doctor, lets him tell her this is normal, that her sister must not be allowed to stay in bed for too long, that she will perhaps have another child soon. That these things are not fathomable, that some people think they are the will of God – but he sees her face and stops.

'And do you have something to occupy you?' he asks.

Cooking, cleaning, throwing food out, sleeping, shitting, proofreading, washing Sandra's clothes, washing Sandra, feeding Sandra, washing Ellen's clothes, feeding Ellen, washing Ellen's hair. Washing her own clothes, they should be the cleanest women in the country, washing the floors, sweeping.

'No,' he says, very gently. 'I mean, what do you enjoy doing?'

Jocelyn thinks she has lost her understanding of language; perhaps this is what happens when a person starts to die from the inside out.

'What did you used to enjoy?' he says, coaching her.

She cannot answer. Thinks of Martin; and the imaginary garden comes into her head. They both seem very far away.

'Work,' she says.

He smiles, picks up his piece of paper and passes it to her. 'Then you should try to get back into your work. To get back into things.'

Later she takes the little brown bottles from her handbag, putting one on Ellen's bedside table and taking the other to her bathroom cabinet. When she puts the pill in her mouth after lunch she remembers the doctor and looks out the window at the garden. The dogwood has died.

The Valium makes a garden in her blood, she thinks. That is enough.

It is seven weeks since the baby.

She is into the second-last volume of the encyclopaedia now, forcing herself through it daily, page by page, noting, scribbling, punctuating. Only this evening has she once more begun to properly read the words.

In the rainforests of Carnarvon Gorge, inland Queensland, is the largest native rock art site in the country. The ochre handprints are testament to the primitive presence of the Aborigine.

This morning in the kitchen Ellen told her she was going back to London.

Jocelyn stared at her, silent, then said, 'You can't take Sandra back there.'

Then Ellen had said, her voice tainted with disgust – the first evidence of emotion in seven weeks – 'What, *you'll* look after her?'

They faced each other. Neither woman any longer felt

the urge to cry. Ellen walked into the living room to the telephone.

Jocelyn stood on the green linoleum staring into the kitchen sink, listening to Ellen's voice talking to the travel agent. Staring at the small digs and dints in the white enamel, Jocelyn stood.

When she heard Ellen speak again she went in and touched her arm: 'I'm coming with you.'

Ellen narrowed her eyes for an instant, then shrugged. Turning her gaze back to the faded pink flowers of the carpet, she said into the receiver, 'Actually, it's three seats.'

Afterwards Jocelyn returned to the manuscript, to the hand-prints of Carnarvon Gorge. High on the rock face, those perfect outlined hand-prints, of men, mothers, children. Families. The pale red hand its own silent language, there among the glittering green and the squawks of the birds dropped down from the air.

At nine o'clock in the evening it is her turn for the telephone.

In Pittwater the ringing carries out and out, across the black lapping water. Martin answers at last; then, after she tells him, they listen to the clicks and hisses of the telephone wire, each holding tight to the receiver, the black plastic, like driftwood for the drowning.

PART TWO

martin
1964

Nineteen

A NTHONY STANDS AT his counter and dries a water glass with a cloth. Through the window he watches the new one – quiet, not so young – moving between the buildings. Walking with slow steps the path around the cloister (such as it is, more school quadrangle than holy place).

They are all scrubbed clean of their stories by the time they get here. At first they had been mostly pale, slow Irish boys whose families had delivered them from Dublin streets to Dublin brothers. One son a parish priest, the other a Trappist – but never suspecting their boy might be torn from his country like that, not understanding that a promise to a monastery meant to go where you were sent, agree to be dragged across oceans to the bottom of the earth, towards God.

Anthony was the first Australian boy to come. And

through the decades since his own arrival, the infirmarian has watched the same shock play out across their faces in the first weeks. The real shock of being woken in the dark, breathless with a pounding heart, the waking they would never get used to. The shock of walking on gravel under the cold stars for Vigils and then Lauds in the dawn. And the screeching, screaming white birds with wingspans like arms that circle the black trees beyond their dormitory rooms.

It's the shock of bending not to a soft dark kneeler hollowed by the centuries of other men's knees, but to new-hewn wood that even after twenty years still splinters the skin and smells of the strange gaseous trees of this land. The shock of a monastery's prayer only held together by clapboard, and of the blinding sun on baking earth outside.

And nothing to contemplate out there but the bone-yellow Australian plains, the flat, bleached blue sky, the sound of mattock thudding into tussock, or striking iron stone and juddering in their hands. And they try to suppose that Christ could live here, though it horrors their hearts to think of it.

But the greatest shock for any of them, he knows, is the silence – by order of the abbot and St Benedict. Of having your own tongue stilled inside your mouth, the better to listen for God.

So. It's this that brings each one in time to Brother Anthony's infirmary door, and he tends to them, as they stare about at the white beds and the grey curtains, the smell of Epsom salts finding their nostrils. He shuffles between them, offering bed rest and tea and hot-water bottles, and then they realise they have the chance to speak. For austere conversation is permitted with him, the infirmarian, but by this time the silence has woven itself in with the shock, and often it is only when they have recovered and he is opening the door for them to leave that they want to tell him their stories, those lives peeled off them before they entered here.

But once they know it's possible, they store their speaking up and deliver it to him with their ailments. He does not ever tell them he's heard all their lives before, from other flat-faced boys just like themselves.

Obedience, humility, perseverance. Shovelling shit over the fence from the dusty earth of the sheep yards, Martin does not know why he is here, does not care. It is a relief to be told: walk there, wear this (a flapping dress, absurd, he does not care), sing this, sleep, eat.

He shovels each raked grey pile into the barrow, hitches his habit up to move, lifts another shovelful of pebbled sheep shit. In this mindless repetition he thinks he is supposed to pray. The idea is ludicrous. He lets his brain fall still.

If he tries to think of his arrival here – a week ago, a month? – it is as some watery delirium, or dream. A leather chair, the abbot's hand. Perhaps he cried. Later, being led to one narrow iron bed in a row of twenty, then one space in the choir-stall among the rows of others, one refectory chair, one plate, one cup.

There were the months after Jocelyn left. When all he could think to do was walk into the bush and disappear. And then, with the entire supply of the surgery's morphine and some opiated instinct, a train trip south, then west. Occasionally, out through the windows over those rhythmic days and nights, he stared into a stunned Hereford's glossed, resiny eyes, its turned head looming from the dark. He had walked into a pub, legs moving as though he had been months at sea. The weeks in the town, the morphine running out and crying into the sheets for Jocelyn's sleep-flung hand over his hip.

And now there is the silence, as he kneels and works and walks and sleeps.

Anthony watches him, knows the buried baby is what haunts this Martin's mind, kneeling there in the yellow-lit chapel or stalking out across the paddocks. They have all heard how he was found up on the ridge that day, inco-herent by the unknown baby's grave. And Anthony has seen him since, returning across the flats in the early mornings. When Martin is absent from the abbey, Anthony knows it is that old child's grave at which he kneels to offer his Psalms.

We are all lonely, brother.

In the beginning, Anthony knows, their heads are bursting full of words, and in church the Psalms come rushing out, all words and noise, all need and desire and relief.

Anthony thinks he can see the shape of their need in the first weeks, and it is all shaped like women. They scandalise themselves, they find the Psalms have hips and breasts and they arch backwards into prayer that smells of women, is soft as women. And they think it is any woman they want, but in the infirmary Anthony sees their faces when they're released into a dreaming sleep, and they're each crying for their own mother.

When Anthony arrived here in 1930 he felt the Irishmen's cold gaze on him and their brimstone hearts harden against him. But standing there on the porch with his bag heavy at his shoulder he turned and looked around him at the scraped land, at the sky bluer than any Irish air, and he thought, *This is my country*; and he stared those old men down, and set his bag on the cold verandah stone.

He liked to work with the sheep, it reminded him of home, and then he liked to walk in the frosty dark to

Vigils still caught in the slow web of sleep. Then he learned the sign language and learned to trust those peaceful things coming into him, he thinks from the Virgin, and he is able to believe now in the love of God almost all the time.

A bout of influenza, then pneumonia, had brought him to the infirmary in '42 and kept him here for three months. Where he began to learn the rhythms of old Ignatius's bottles and herbs and when and why he used them. After which the old man kept him there in training.

From this infirmary he has watched the tides and circles of the novice year. It moves on, the shock disappears, their faces turn brown with work in the sun, their forearms grow sinewed, and lustful thoughts subside.

The only fullness left there then is the wish still to talk. Sometimes Anthony thinks that this is what becomes of desire in a monastery: all need turns into only the desire to speak.

So they read the Psalms.

I am poured out like water, and all my bones are out of joint: my heart is like wax; it is melted in the midst of my bowels.

In his student days, when morphine was only for pleasure, Martin liked to take a tiny amount and then walk around the steep edges of the Pittwater beach. He is reminded of it in the cloister, on the third day of the fast in this, his first year. Of the way that clear, slow glaze had formed over his vision, the seaweeded rocks becoming blood splotches beneath the water.

He is enjoying this wandering of his mind, those images, lost for so long, returning desiccated, but somehow more intense.

He is interested too in the physiology, and the illusory psychology, of the fast. The lightheadedness, the tilting of the room if he moves too quickly. The intensification of the senses over the days, so that he can smell laundry soap on the clothes of Anthony where he sits reading, though he is eleven feet from the open window, inside the infirmary. This hypersensitivity disconnects Martin from himself. Watching, he wonders if this is what it feels like to die, this effervescent, aerial stroking away from the physical, sensory world. When the senses are so sprawl-ing, so easily released, sent out like streamers or homing birds, returning with a distant scent, the sound of scraping mud from boots on the neighbouring farm . . . and then he knows it, in the short hard spaces of concentration, as delirium. What he imagines as some kind of god takes visceral, sculptural form, and almost, once, speaks. And Martin can even attempt what he thinks might be prayer: it is like swimming in green water. Cool, easy, progres-sive, nearing something clear and sharp.

This ease will sink rapidly away when he once again has that electrical weight, the massive bulk – of bread, or pea – on his tongue. But it is as though the deprivation of food sets the fuse for every sense but hunger, which only lies dully, unrecognised, at the base of all the other fissuring, hissing and popping machinations of the nerve endings.

And, inevitably, Jocelyn. She comes singing into his body, all fern-frond hair and smooth eucalyptical limbs, all dank, androgynous arousal, rising from the coastal rainforest or the marshes of western New South Wales. She is cross-continental, bicoastal, vampiric as she comes to him on these yellow plains.

He dreams then that she is in Spain, makes her flamenco and castanet like a clacking souvenir doll. His tongue is sticking to the roof of his mouth. He drinks water carefully, moves slowly, in stages as though learning for the first time to move, tests his weight on his hands, the balls of his feet, gets down to kneel. Prays her, stumbling, from his mind.

After these decorated hallucinations the cool clarity of the infirmary comes to him as relief. Washed out, still a little lightheaded, it is a comfort to rejoin the conscious presence of another human being and the stark wooden light. Martin breathes deeply as he lies there, but keeps his eyes open, not wanting a return, yet, to those shifting images.

'St Bernard prescribed prayer and love alone for the sick,' the infirmarian, Anthony, tells him, screwing the lid on a jar. Then laughs softly, a guttural sound. 'I don't know how well that worked,' he says. Then sniffs his fingers.

The football dressing-room smell of liniment recalls for Martin his university days again. Another roomful of men.

'St Bernard thought there was nothing but trouble in medicine. That to seek relief from disease in medicine was in harmony neither with our religion nor with the purity of the order. Odd, do you think?'

Martin is still stunned by the sound of the man's voice, its confidence, its volume. He nods, not hearing the words, only their noise, the sharpness of the loudly spoken air outside the chapel. He himself has not spoken for weeks, only responding to another novice's unlawful, urgent whisper with nods or shrugs.

Now he traces back, follows Anthony's speech about Bernard, the Abbey of Cîteaux built on a swamp. About the prohibited study of medicine. Martin imagines his university professors laughing to see him here, sitting under the clumsy hands of a halfwit man-nurse administering wives'-tale poultices like a child slapping mud pies.

Shaking their heads at his wasted years in the lecture halls, the anatomy lab, the hospitals.

The infirmary smells of carbolic acid and Dettol, has the metallic sound of kidney dishes and shoe squeaks on linoleum. The first time he came in here it was a home-coming of the senses, but he dreamed of the baby for nights afterwards. Of that moment, the slippery weight in his hands, over and over.

Anthony washes his hands at the sink in the corner, waiting for Martin to speak, this sallow young man, quicker-eyed than most. Anthony has noticed that Martin watches his movements too closely, like an examiner.

He has noticed, too, across the yards and at mealtimes, that Martin has seemed not to take to the sign language. The other novices learn quickly enough the monastery's ancient language of the fingers. The hands of some move in the air like smoke, like dancing steam. There are even jokes, curled with deft fingers when the novice master's back is turned. It's only strictly meant for work. *Help me*, or *stop*. It is not the language men carry in their hearts; but their hearts' language is supposed to be kept for God.

The young monks finger sentences to one another across the cloister, behind the covers of books when they're filing in for the reading, the *Lectio Divina*. In the garden, and beyond, fluttering fingers across paddocks and from beneath tractors and across the snufflings of pigs in the sty. Desperate dances of fingers to reveal their selves to one another.

Except for this Martin, this young man floating upwards out of his delirium and dehydration, carefully watching everything, walking the perimeters, but leaving unlearned the language of the hands.

Once during Anthony's early years he heard a boy cry out *Take me home*, this cry, *Mama, bring me home*, and under-blanket stifled sobs and sobs to follow. But in the morning he saw the young brother's face had set to stone from grief. It was as though all need had flowed out of the boy in the night and now he was ready to wait for God.

Later it was tuberculosis, not the Holy Spirit, that descended into the boy and dwelt there, and by the time it came to the end he was simply tired out with waiting. His twenty-four-year-old eyes watched past the rites read him by the abbot, heard the wheeling of that white cockatoo screaming into his morning dreams, and Anthony knew it was the bird's shriek, not the peace of God, which went with that boy into death.

It was the first burial Anthony saw here, the lowering of a friend wrapped only in his habit into the stony grave.

When Ignatius died ten years later, Anthony had washed the old man's body and, as he moved him a last, leftover breath had come out, as though to say *Do not cry,*

I am here. But it was only physiology, that exhalation, not life. And Anthony had sat by the bed until morning and held Ignatius's dead hand in his, thinking, *I cannot go on.*

Ignatius, who had taught him about healing scabs and setting bones and bringing down fevers and liniments for a scald. Who taught him more than his own mother did about love, about love.

For a year or more, he could kneel and pray only to Ignatius, could not believe in anything less substantial. In the infirmary, everything had been touched by the old man's hands.

He could pray only one prayer then, one sentence – from the Song of Songs, but in Anthony's mind it was only ever in Ignatius's phlegmy voice:

Set me as a seal on your heart, for love is stronger than death.

He moves across the dark linoleum to the young Martin, lying there in the narrow white bed. Who wanders the ridge when he should be working, who fasts without permission, who is bloated up with grief. Anthony holds him out a cup of tea, sets it down on the bedside cabinet.

And as he leans he whispers, 'Do not cry, I am here.'

The young man, this Martin, stares at him and then under his breath mutters something Anthony cannot hear, but he knows it is meant like a slap to his face. He holds Martin's hand in both of his for a moment, then smoothes the bedclothes.

Love is stronger than death.

Twenty

WHEN MARTIN HAS recovered from his fast he moves back into the dormitory, away from the smells of disinfectant to those of farts and bedclothes, to the snoring and the scratchings, the grunts and wheezes of forty sleeping men. And to those things not spoken of in the confessional: the dark urgent breath of a young man drowning in lust and loneliness, the whimpers of dreams.

In the dormitory he misses the clean light of the infirmary. He had begun to enjoy watching the infirmarian's hocus-pocus each day, his little bottles, his handfuls of herbs, as though antibiotics have not been invented. His breathless leaning over the mortar and pestle like some jowly apprentice. Martin does not dwell on that moment's warmth in the man's rough hands over his.

Oysters. Inexplicably, obscenely, and after all this time, he has a craving for oysters here in the weak winter morning's sunlight. Ice still feathers the ground in the shade, and beads of melted frost pool on the sills where he is washing the library windows.

Once at Pittwater they had borrowed a small boat and motored up the Hawkesbury to a tiny green beach and levered oysters from the rocks. At the edge where the bush met the sand they had sat together, prising and gouging at the ancient grey forms, bending their butter knives. Then the soft popping click as each one opened and the oyster, silver-green on the blind white shell. Taking one into his mouth to taste all the ocean rocks and beaches of New South Wales.

She had lain on the blanket and he'd caught a whiting, walked to her holding the invisible line high in one hand, the fish arching and moving at the end of it. She'd been sorry for it, its distressed flapping. And he showed her the effortless death, the sudden blind butt between its eyes with the handle of the knife. He had gone back to cast the line again into the waves. When the fish was still she watched it closely, said it was 'a beautiful silver thing', wanted to take a photograph of it.

But then it had revived, and begun flapping, half-crawling, on its side. She'd called him back to the *poor thing*, then looked away as he'd tried again to kill it, in the end ashamed, stabbing it roughly with a knife, gashed and blood-covered.

That afternoon they sat among the trees in the falling dusk drinking beer from a bottle, and they stared around them, listening and watching the ticking undergrowth.

He thinks the men here would say the *presence* that day was something sacred, that God was the reason for their silence there, being surrounded by Him. Martin had thought it was only the painted glass curtains of the bush, on and on, enclosing them. But now, remembering, he feels a shift, wonders if perhaps there was something holy there.

But in the next second his fingers are only cold and sueded from the newsprint, and there is nothing sacred, he is only a window-washer in the cold light of this blighted farm. He is a tussock-puller, flagstone-scrubber, a drudge for somebody's idea of a god, and in the evenings when he reads their holy books his eyes blur and layer the lines of type, the letters lift away from the paper and slide over one another, and he clenches his jawbone to stay awake.

In the evenings Martin reads. He meditates on the words. What does it mean, to meditate? What does the word mean? He walks the spindly weatherboarded cloister around the darkening rose garden. Words rise up and spread out in his mind, their parts mixing and unscrambling like Scrabble squares. He thinks his intellect is failing him, falling into disuse.

By the second year he craves a dictionary. Not the library Oxford, to which he sneaks in the evenings with his pile of remembered words. He can't retain all the definitions in his mind, or return to them when he needs to. Or else the definitions are meaningless. *Cloister*: a covered walk, esp. of a monastery or church. *Faith*: confidence or trust in a person or thing. He wants a dictionary of his own, to own a dictionary, an elaborate, many-volumed, personal, only-for-his-eyes dictionary. Once he would have laughed out loud, and hard, at the idea of this being the thing to fantasise about for months on end. Not sex, nor cigarettes, nor brandy. Not coffee. Not the feel of money in your fingers. Not even speech, now.

A dictionary that told you something of what you looked for.

He is sick from wishing.

There is a railway track through the property, and the men pause sometimes as they work, listening to the train at their backs, trying not to imagine the people inside, those wives and children they will never have. The lives they will not see, returning from simple journeys they will never make.

In the paddocks at marking each year the lambs gather in nervous clutches with the sheep. The wind is icy across the flats and the iron cradle is freezing even through his gloves. What St Francis would make of it. Men in robes and working aprons, tackling lambs with all the weight of their bodies into the dry dust of the sheep yards, forcing them kicking and braying into the cradle for mutilation, the anxious mothers waiting beside the fence. The stunned lambs skittering drunkenly once thrown onto the grass, stumbling and bloody. A murderous scene, the men head to foot in blood, the medieval whine of the cradle, the shocked animals, tipped out as bloodied rubbish.

Martin used to think medicine was about knowledge, and faith about ignorance. Under the weak Australian winter sun, all intellect sunken away, he wonders why Christian men have not believed in that foreign word, *karma*.

At the end of the day he can't lift a teapot. His shoulders burn. It is more difficult still to kneel in the abbey, with the smell of the animals' cut organs uncleaned from him despite the scrubbing. Once again he does not know why he is here. If he has ever had a reason that is speakable.

The next morning he must do it all again. He is hungry, in time with the stomach squirls of Matthias next to him. In the abbey he abandons prayer. Lets out his stomach, rests his head on his empty folded hands and listens to the shrieks of the cockatoos slinging themselves across the white sky outside, and waits quietly for that other possibility. Belief.

Anthony watches Martin through the early years, his hands unspeaking still, his wanderings up through the bush to the ridge. At the desk beside him in the scriptorium in the evenings Anthony reads Genesis again, but some nights the words evade him and he uses the stillness to look around at the other men. Turning pages with fingers calloused from shovelling, or milking, or holding fence posts or sledge-hammering them in. Fingers clasping over the knuckles of their own other hand while they wait for God to answer them from the paper. And sometimes two cupped hands will make a private cradle for a young or old man's face, just resting there a while from exhaustion or confusion or homesickness, a cradle latticed with dark and flesh-coloured light, and all the things that writhe slowly through the hours of a monastery's day.

Yet at times he has watched it grow: an understanding of a reason to be here, settling into a man like peace. It is in the warmth of one man's hand on another's shoulder while they carry firewood, or in one slowing his footsteps to walk in time with his friend. When Anthony feels his own reason to stay, it is like swimming. And it is the rhythm of the swimming itself, not how far it takes him, that gives him certainty.

As Anthony works in the infirmary's laundry, boiling the sheets, he daydreams about the Tree of Knowledge, as he used to when a child.

What a tree that must have been. Vast, and stretching skywards, gold-encrusted, and lava flowing down it, and hanging in its branches visions of all human history's ideas. What a cacophony! With the birds, and insects climbing in and out of all invention. Think of it: the Eiffel Tower, and now rocket ships, and electricity, and the telegraph, and inventions of every other kind – radio waves, and cosmic photographing instruments. And it must have spread the size of a continent, at least, to hold all human knowledge in its limbs.

The water boils. Anthony pokes the sheets under with a stick, and thinks of all the languages of the tree, and all Leonardo's art, Picasso's, and all of New York City, the ships to get there, all the wars and all religions of the world sprouted there on its limbs. And trigonometry, and Marie Curie's spectacular hatchings. Yes, and DNA helixes, and antibiotics, and my God, did they see atomic explosions, Hiroshima burning, in it? In this tree, the tree of all knowledge?

And those two poor new-made fools standing beneath it, bamboozled.

He lifts the sheets out with the stick, steam filling the room. Thinks of Martin breathing next to him in the scriptorium, head bent over a book, frowning.

Anthony hefts the steaming sheets into the wringer. It does not concern him that none of them will ever know anything. He thinks bamboozlement is a sort of grace.

Twenty-One

A CROP DUSTER DRONES overhead, on its way to who knows where, dropping fertiliser or something else to rain down on the land. At the water pump Martin is sweating, though now in the midst of a year-old drought the air is drier than ever. Anthony has told him there is a mouse plague in the northern states. The plane scours the sky overhead, above these times of famine and plague and strange raining air.

Those years ago when he worked in Sydney the city was scandalised one silver afternoon by a harebrained pilot flying his Cessna under the Harbour Bridge on a dare. 'Just like drivin' a car,' the young man drawled later, when he'd landed on a Griffith farmer's airstrip. Grinning for the local paper with a piece of rice stalk sticking from his mouth and braces holding up his trousers. The rice-farmer clapping his back and laughing. *'The best pilot since Pontius,'* *said Griffith farmer Mr Alex Downey*, read the caption.

Anthony has told him there is only one novice entering this year. 'A different kind of drought,' he had said, peering at a yellow dishcloth in his hand after wiping dust from his dark glass bottles over the sink.

Martin had not answered, but returned to his rosary, counting the years and the months and the days he has been here. Wondering about the shape of the world now beyond the boundaries of this particular knobbled blur of earth.

He remains fearful of the gloom of the dormitory in which he still wakes amid the muffled noises of the sleeping men. Most remembrances have long ago begun to fail him. Sandra's face, and Ellen's, have turned opaque. The road to the mountains house has become any road he ever drove. Even Jocelyn's face fades in and out sometimes. But this other unwanted image still rises clear and strong. A perfectly formed dead child held naked in his hands, glistening and warm from his mother's slowly breathing body. Over the years in his dreams that weight has become a stone, or water, or seaweed, or earth. Anything but that sweet wet armful of someone else's lifeless child.

He takes this memory with him when he visits the old hillside grave, buries it there with his prayers every time.

Twenty-Two

LENTEN WINDS COME sailing over the paddocks. Thistling for the seventeenth day. The mattock thuds into the earth, he levers it with calloused fingers and palm-flesh, the musty blade tears at the stubble's roots. Thuds, then tears. Thuds, then tears. Thuds, then tears. Takes a step. Thuds, then tears.

More than four years here and he thinks he may be beginning to know the edges of a vast god.

In the evenings he climbs the ridge to history, to the baby's grave. Gets to his knees and sits there on his haunches, enclosed among the trees and breathing in the earthy air. He thinks he may have learnt what it means to pray, here. But still he asks the air for the thing he knows he cannot have.

Coming down the hill he sees young Frank, sweeping the porch, watching him. He tries to catch Martin's eye as they file into the abbey.

Martin ignores him. This new boy is particularly annoying, he moons around after one brother then another, flattering them in schoolboy whispers, offering bits of gossip. No doubt he has been thrilling the others with news of Martin's wanderings in the bush, despite the abbot's latest warnings.

Days later, chipping weed from the paddocks, Martin sees Frank bobbing nearer to him across the dead flat. He keeps working, silent. The boy is at his side, smiling, dropping his mattock lightly to the earth, moving about in a mime of work.

His fingers flicker, signing to Martin that he wishes he had a secret place to pray like that. The dark band of the bush ridge rises up behind Frank's sweep of arm. Martin stares. But decides the boy is all speculation and false humility, and ignores this invitation.

He straightens up to toss the thistles into the barrow.

Frank leans in, turning his head to look Martin in the eye, whispers, 'I envy you.'

Martin breathes, turns from the barrow, closes his eyes. Swings the mattock high, and it comes down cutting hard into the earth. Oblivious, Frank is still talking: he cannot be as true a brother as Martin, he has too many doubts, is not as strong in his faith.

Carefully swinging the mattock, Martin begins therosary, loudly, inside his head. He straightens, meets Frank's gaze and stiffly gestures silence, *work.*

Frank smirks and nods, twirls the mattock pole in his hands. And then, keeps on: he cannot speak to the abbot on this matter, prayer does not help. 'You could help me, though, perhaps, if we could talk.'

Martin, all quiet fury now, lifts dead thistles with his hands into the barrow. And then lifts the barrow handles, pushing it striding over the paddock away from the boy's whining voice.

Frank smiles after him with his pale blank face, then the smile falls away, and he turns, listless, back to his mattock.

At Vespers Martin sees him across the gold light given off by the pine pews. Closes his eyes, prays the stupid boy's face from him. Opens his eyes and sees Frank open-mouthed, singing about him like a child. Feels tightening in his jaw.

Another afternoon, at the henhouse, stooping in under the roosts for the eggs, Frank starts up. 'It's a sin, I know. But really it's just admiration. I don't understand how that can be a sin?'

Martin mumbles to himself about the eggs. He turns and chickens flail upwards. The dusty air.

Handing the warm eggs over to the young brother he sees the raised, adoring face.

'I mean, it's a good thing, isn't it? I can learn from watching you. Everything being so easy for you. In the nicest way.'

Frank is confidential, twittering, flirting. *He's fucking blushing.*

Martin knows that any god should strike him dead for what he does next, does not care. The witless Frank held swaying in the chicken wire, the smoking air, Martin's snarling into the boy's face – hears the years of silent rage in his own voice: 'EASY! Just fuck off, you pathetic little shit. Go home.'

Poor Frank's mulleted face, his stupid child's eyes springing tears, sprawling in the chicken dirt, the dropped eggs broken yellow pools in the dust, his habit rucked above his adolescent knees.

Martin spends hours in silent shuddering, begging forgiveness down on his knees, in private, in the church. Wishing away the words, the hands round the boy's thin shoulders. Knowing Frank will never forgive him, Jesus, God will never forgive him.

He has wasted four years, was getting so close.

And now what?

Frank, sniffily, comes to him months later. Says he has found it in his heart, with God's help, he draws it out, the abbot has helped him . . . to forgive him. And Martin gets down on his knees in the grassy dust, kissing the hand of this silly boy who may be his salvation.

Twenty-Three

T HE VEGETABLE GARDENER, James, is angular and large-footed in his steel-capped black boots, an older hand even than Martin, who has been sent here to obey his directions.

It seems he is too proud, is spending too much time alone, he has been seen *again* walking the ridge, the novice master (that sniveller) has told him. And so he stands at the garden gate, waiting to be communal, and humbled.

In the refectory, where boredom and silence make hungry men lose their manners, he has watched James. Because in a silent place even chewing becomes an activity. And staring. They all do it, except the odd new arrival who remains polite for a few weeks, until the silence gets to him and he too makes his body's facilities become interesting. Martin can register every movement of his own eyeballs now, he counts them, maps the path of his shifting iris, sometimes makes himself giddy in this cartography. Or he takes his own pulse, the only shred of ritual left from those long ago days when he thought his hands could heal.

Across the tables he has watched them all. Anthony, that talking infirmarian, gabbler, who eats too fast, looking about him as though willing someone to speak. Matthias, who works on his chewing as though it is a job, staring at the breadboard, his great filthy fingers curled in fists around his knife and fork. He eats with his mouth open, breathing in disgusting catarrhal snorts. It was in the refectory that the realisation came one day, some time back, that this life had acquainted Martin with hatred.

He has his refectory portraits of them all. And James picks out his bread with too much care, he smiles, his fingernails are clean. He makes Martin feel decayed.

Now in the autumn air, leaning over the garden gate, Martin exhales, closes his eyes. For the thousandth time he thinks of leaving. Of finding his way back to Jocelyn and the garden in her head. And then, instantly, as always, of the sickening truth of her being lost, not wanting him.

James's hand is on his arm and the smooth neck of a garden fork slapped into his palm.

Obedience, humility, perseverance. *Hate your own will,* wrote Benedict.

James directs him to dig up the far garden bed and prepare it for planting; it has been untouched since last summer. At first he uses the fork, but after a time he can see the only way to remove all the weeds is to use small movements with the fingers, grasping the base of a weed. After its turning, the soil is soft, the weeds come easily away. *Pick, pick.*

He watches James at another bed from the corner of his eye, on his hands and knees, dibbing holes for seedlings.

There is nothing masculine about this duty here. Pick, pick.

Except the silence, perhaps.

But then the graziers on nearby properties are allowed large gestures, shouts, curses, kicks even, at a dog or a gate. They swagger, they flap their hats at flies, at the sun, and sweat sheens their skin. Despite the hats they are red- and rough-skinned, their hands, even wrists, thickened with callouses. He shifts and kneels again in the soil, his hands beginning to perspire in the welder's gloves. Pick, pick. The straw hat has become heavy. He crouches and removes the gloves. He kneels forward again, plucks at weeds with his fingers, thumb and forefinger, lifting and sinking as though he is sewing, embroidering the earth with the gestures of a woman, or a surgeon.

When he studied medicine he had practised his sutures in the furniture of his house. An old girlfriend had stood outside one night, watching through the window at the movements of his wrist and hand as he knelt on the couch. Like a ballet, she had said. His chairs, couches, cushions, curtains, all sutured with transparent thread to his shining future.

He looks up to see James sitting on his haunches, watching him. Their eyes meet and then each turns back to his work.

He tips a barrow of sheep shit into the soil, fetches the fork again. Foot on iron, forces it into earth, and lifts and turns the soil clods.

Sexual need runs through this place sometimes like a shiver. His own desire has become a weed through his sleep. He has dreamt of that old girlfriend, of the needle in his fingers. He dreamt he sewed her to himself. In the morning he realised he had ejaculated in his sleep. Is not ashamed, they cannot make him that. But his need wearies and bores him. *Our Father, Who art in heaven.* It is common, he knows; these thoughts happen to everyone.

But still, after all these years, during these needy nights it is mostly Jocelyn in his bed.

He pushes the thought away, again puts a foot to the iron shelf of the fork. Whispers the prayer inside his head, begins again. Reminds himself that every minute

Twenty-Four

BEHIND THE BUILDING is the view from the verandah – the pale valley, the dark velvet ring of reeds and rushes around the dam. It is not visible to him. He walks, circling the rose garden, watching the grey cement path and the appearance, disappearance, appearance of his black boots from beneath the skirts of his habit. The roses list over the dust-dry earth. The doubt, always only just dormant, rises through him like a temperature. Is it possible to believe in something one cannot understand?

He walks. He wishes he could see the valley. He watches the same tough straggle of rosebush as he passes it. He sits, for a while, under the awning covering the cloister walk, reading. Or rather, tracing the pattern of marks of ink on the page with the movement of his eyes, comparing the way some letters bleed more heavily into the paper than others. *H*, for example, seems to sink more thoroughly into the paper than *A*. He breathes, slowly, this dry air and the heat of the place contained in this breath. Then in this breath.

He thinks of Jocelyn's fantasised garden, of her somewhere – still in England? In Europe? – standing amid a field of plants, without him. Forces his mind away from this, yet again, and stands. He shakes his head quickly, violently, as he used to do when driving long distances to keep himself awake. He walks, tries to turn his mind to God. Whatever this word might mean.

Later, as he's walking up the hillside to the old grave with the letter in his pocket, he wonders why he has written it. He has long ago understood there are some things for which forgiveness is not possible. He did not ask for it.

Dear Jocelyn. Her written name so unfamiliar now, only her face unforgettable. Are she and Ellen together, still, with Sandra? He imagines Sandra. She would be much older now, though it is impossible for him to say how many years have passed. Does she remember him, the doctor who let her brother die?

He has said barely anything in the letter, only where he is, and *sorry*, and something Anthony told him, from the Song of Songs.

The season shifts again and it is hot, and the sheep start, then stumble away across the stony ground as he walks up the hill. One bleats a guttural, low groan, some others repeat the sound in another key.

The fence around the little grave is rusted in parts. He has not been here for some months, since the day he wrote to her. He will paint the fence soon. He climbs over it and kneels on the cement, begins grasping at the base of the weeds around the grave, then starts to heap them in the centre of the cement. He makes a rosary of the weeds. *Hail Mary full of Grace*, aloud, 'The Lord is with Thee,' digging the roots out with his fingers. After some time the words themselves become soothing.

The letter was sent many months ago and nothing has come back. He is not surprised. He had written only a guessed-at street name, a London suburb, remembered from those old blue letters from Thomas.

He should not have written to her, reviving that old need. Her silence is not a surprise, but still he feels the small hard mass of a cry beginning in his chest for the first time since he arrived here those years ago. He sits on the cement grave with his face in his hands.

Twenty-Five

ANTHONY RISES IN the dark, as he does every morning, feels around the cupboard for his clothes. He does not turn on the light. He has come to love darkness, knows the spaces of his room and its furnishings – bed, desk, cupboard and drawers – like the mathematics of his own body. Quickly dressed, he likes to scurry to the abbey for Vigils before the others get there. He begins his prayer before he sees another man's face, before the lights are lit. These are the times he is most able to believe in God, and in love. Just after waking from sleep, and just before falling into it. When perhaps life is most like dying.

In the vegetable garden James hands Martin a palm-sized river stone on which he has carved a Latin word. *Colo.*

Martin's schoolboy language lessons fail him. He holds the stone in his hand and looks at James, shakes his head.

'It means both –' James says – 'cultivate, and worship.'

Martin nods. He signs, *Beautiful.* Rests the stone on the low wall around the onion bed, they both stand to look at it. So poetry can grow among the weeds and the mistakes and the onion sprouts. Then James smiles and walks back between the beds to return to the composting heap.

Martin watches his shoulders move beneath his habit, and he realises that for the first time in years, in this unaccountable moment, he is feeling it: love.

One early morning after rain they are finding snails and crushing them on the concrete paths. It is an easy triumph, the fight against the snails simpler and more final than against the daily destruction by wallabies and kangaroos, the rabbits, the great holes dug by a disoriented wombat. Against these they build fortresses of fences, surround the lettuce plants with barbed wire and broken glass.

'And people think a garden is a gentle place,' James whispers to him, standing rueful, looking at the traps protecting their food.

He looks up to Martin, smiling, waiting.

And suddenly Martin is talking about Jocelyn and her

Twenty-Six

THEY WALK TOGETHER to the rubbish tip, wheelbarrowing the monastery's refuse. Tin cans, cardboard flour boxes. Wheat bags, an old metal bucket with holes rusted in its base. A chair repaired so many times and now irreparable. They stand sorting the rubbish into anything reusable. James takes what he can for the compost, for mulch. Over the year they have learned one another's rhythms, they work companionably for an hour, lifting, bending, sorting. James tries now and then to sign to Martin. He shrugs in return, not understanding.

They work. The sun lifts in the blue air. James walks to the fence and watches Martin shovelling rubbish into the pit. Martin sees him then, leaning over the fence post, head in his hands. He walks over to him. James is trembling, shamed. Martin puts his hand on his shoulder. The man turns around. *I know*, Martin says. *I know*.

He holds his hands out, James takes them. Then James's face is close, his hands are shaking and he is kissing and kissing Martin's soft and tender mouth.

It is a poorly fenced yellow paddock under a blue sky beside a pale dirt road. Inside the fence, beside the old but well-kept gate with its mended hinges, is a white wooden shelter. Inside the shelter is a simple wooden bench, where guests who do not drive here sit waiting for the bus back to town.

Turning from the grave one morning, through the eucalypts, Martin thinks he sees the figure of a man climb into the bus. It heaves away down the road, leaving the dust and the sound of its changing gears hanging in the air behind it.

That evening James is not at dinner. His chair has disappeared and the brothers have been instructed to move their chairs so as to fill the space. When they retire the novices all walk past the space where his bed has been in the dormitory. The bed is waiting for removal in the corridor, mattress stripped, the blankets folded in neat squares in a stack on the corner of the grey ticking. They see it. They avoid each other's looks. No one signs James's name with their fingers as they exchange goodnights.

It is a kind of unmentionable death.

Twenty-Seven

A GARDEN IS NOT a gentle place, James had whispered to him.

Since he has gone Martin thinks constantly of Eden, and Gethsemane, those places of serpents and betrayal. He finds himself crying quite often now, and wondering why it is that he does not leave. He tries to pray.

He thinks of war. He heard from a brother who went into town to the dentist that there is a war in Asia, and that Australian men are being sent there to fight.

His father was in the medical corps on the Kokoda Trail. When the child Martin asked him about it – wanting heroic tales of bullets and snipers and jungle greens – he would never speak of it. Except to talk about the mud, and to say 'it was two steps forward and one slide backwards, all the bloody time'. And that coming home was 'bloody beautiful'.

He thinks he is a coward, perhaps, for not leaving now and joining up. Do they still call it 'joining up'? He thinks of setting foot on the road outside the monastery gate, and then the imagined motion stops. Even a country road is beyond him now. Is this failure of courage the only thing keeping a monastery together?

He knows there is a rifle back at the monastery, in a room near the laundry. Imagines it, the cold tip sharp against the roof of his mouth.

He tries to pray. He prays. He digs, sorts potatoes. He tries to hallucinate the Virgin Mary, Jesus, St Fiacre, the patron saint of gardeners, with his Bible and shovel.

Martin has been sentenced to take over the gardening. He is not supposed to enjoy it. But he kneels at the cauliflower curds to pray and pull weeds, wishing James a better life outside the monastery than he had in it.

'You are to reflect there on what you know of sin,' the abbot tells him. 'You must think hard and ask for God's forgiveness.'

That lunchtime Brother Paul is kneeling in the refectory, holding above his head a broken axe-handle, which had split as he swung the axe down onto the chopping block. His arm wavers. These punishments – the ritualised penance, the public example – are not un-common. Paul, too, was James's friend.

Martin eats slowly, and does not see Frank's smug glance at him across the room.

In the infirmary Anthony lifts the compress away from a novice's boil and dabs it with ointment. They speak about the weather, about Easter. The novice knows better than to ask about James's departure. When a disappearance happens like this, the place divides into the skittish and the still, and this morning Anthony seems barely to be breathing.

The boy is sent on his way with a plaster on his neck, and Anthony washes his hands in hot water at the sink. He holds them there, watching the steam and the colour wash red through his skin. Dries his hands on a cloth by the window, staring down towards the road. He too had watched James climb onto that bus and wished for both their sakes that Martin could be going with him.

Anthony feels the old loss of Ignatius creeping up again, after all these years, like the first swell of nausea. And he takes a deep breath, and prays that this winter will not be a long one.

Holy Thursday, Good Friday, and the chapel sings with incense and the men are all day kneeling, praying the

Stations of the Cross. Once again Martin feels it as a kind of delirium; the sore knees, the aching back are part of him but not, as if he could shrug out of his own skin and float to the rafters to watch himself down here, his falling into grief as Jesus falls on his knees under the weight of the cross.

Last night he read again of Christ at Gethsemane. The garden of death. And as always, in the images that came into Martin's mind, Gethsemane was not the steep foreign place of olive trees and stone but a wide Australian lake, a garden of silver water and broken trees.

He remembers Anthony whispering in his ear those days of his first visit to the infirmary, *Do not cry, I am here.* He had stared up at the man giving him tea and biscuits and shook his head. 'You mean nothing to me,' he had said.

In the chapel on his knees now he is tired and sick of thinking and praying all the time to understand, to lose himself in belief. When any gain is temporary, any decision undone, any faith instantly out of reach. His shoulders hurt. He hauls himself up. It is all he can do to hold onto the pew, and in that moment he decides to release himself. To abandon thought, prayer, feeling. He remembers those first days here, the post-morphine relief at finding someone else steering him through those dead hours between waking and sleep, and he longs again for that surrender of his own will.

But when his body finally meets his bed that night he falls into a deep sleep and in it he dreams of James and Jocelyn, and of that small stone in the vegetable garden and its invocation. Cultivate, and worship.

In the morning he goes to the ledge behind the onion bed and the stone is there. He holds it for a while, and then pushes it into the earth, and as long as it's buried there James is still here, and the baby still lies in its old earth bed among the trees.

Only Jocelyn still sails out there, somewhere, beyond his rest.

PART THREE

Jocelyn
1975

Twenty-Eight

S HE WALKS OUT of her gloomy country hotel into the hard Australian light and across the road into the town's one stock and station agency. The agent is a jocular man in moleskins and riding boots. When she gives him her name, surprise registers on his face.

'I didn't realise you were a woman, from the letter,' he says, and takes his hands from his pockets. He flicks her an up-and-down glance, then begins to talk about his ideas for a country retreat, how he has thought of doing the place up himself over the years. He's known for a long time that the area is ripe for a tourism boom.

Jocelyn stands silent among the sacks of fertiliser and boxes of weed killer, waiting.

The agent smiles at her ruefully. 'But the work in those old buildings,' he says. 'The plumbing alone –' He shuts his mouth as Jocelyn bends in her coat and old trousers over his desk and begins writing a cheque. He goes out into the small back office and takes down from a hook a bunch of keys with a faded red plastic tag.

That same night she drives up the scaly track to the derelict monastery. Too tired to eat, she walks the corridors, which smell of old floor polish and linoleum, until she finds the abbot's room, lies down in a narrow bed in the moonlight and goes to sleep under a small wooden crucifix that imprints itself in her dreams.

In the morning she stands on the porch and scans what she can see of her property. A few stunted rosebushes on mottled grass, a leaning post-and-rail fence, the paddocks beyond stretching out and away. A stagnant dam, then more land until the ridge of bush rises up in the distance, a blackened high wall against the pale yellow of the paddocks. She moves between the buildings, always looking to the treed distance, her eye stopping here and there at a clearing on the encircling ridge.

In the oversized kitchen she unpacks a box of groceries. The entire place is still furnished, though sparsely, and there's a kerosene refrigerator, instead of electric; a wood stove. On the linoleum next to it is a fruit box full of pale kindling pieces, cobwebbed from years of spiders. She tears up the newspaper she has brought with her and begins stuffing the old stove.

Hours later, with a cup of tea and a smoky piece of bread she tours the buildings. The refectory, the laundry. Across the cloister courtyard to the dormitory with its forty pale wooden beds, their grey blankets tucked in tight, like a hospital ward in a war film.

There's surprisingly little dust. She walks through the living rooms, the small visitors' parlour, the scriptorium. Words from an era she does not understand, printed in tiny handwriting on the floor plan in her hands, the deeds of the place in her pocket. Along with Martin's letter, paled with age.

The library with its shelves of books only half-empty, the abbot's office. The echoes, the yellow light of the bathrooms. She hears her own footsteps. Then to the pale infirmary with its high beds and opaque windows and workbench set with bowls and drawers of medicinal tubes and pill bottles. A museum of illness. Did they really live such medieval lives?

She leaves that room, thinking of leeches and its musty smells, keeps walking.

She tries not to think that she is only searching these buildings for signs of him. She moves outside, into the sunlight. Walks among the machinery sheds, the potting shed, the woodshed. Down the path to the abbey; she pushes this door open and the place is flooded with honey light over wooden pews. Moving inside, she sits. Kneels for a minute on the hard wooden plank and rests her chin, on her folded hands, on the back of the pew in front of her.

She stares at the crucifix-shaped white space on the wall above a bare wooden altar.

What is she doing here?

Twenty-Nine

ALMOST THREE YEARS after arriving in England, Jocelyn took the train from London to a Cotswolds village for a job interview.

As she stepped from the Paddington platform onto the train she felt how heavy her body was, how old, how tired from wearing so many heavy clothes. But once past Oxford, the train's windows had filled with a green light. She took off her jacket and leaned towards the window. For the first time she could feel the years of the city's darkness – of typing publishers' rejection letters, answering solicitors' telephones in gloomy offices – dissolving.

Then she was standing on an empty platform and a man was holding out his hand to shake hers. He had dark curly hair, his coat flapped in the wind. His hand was warm.

———

Duncan had been talkative that first Sunday morning. She had sat in the sun on a wooden bench at the rough outdoor table and watched him move back and forth across the garden in his work clothes, digging a trench for drainage pipes, with a green hill rising up beyond him like a picture in a storybook. He called over his shoulder, 'I'll get us lunch in a minute.' It was simple as childhood here, away from London's greasy rain.

Duncan made sandwiches and they ate them from a wooden board with a glass of beer.

She said, 'I feel as though I'm in a painting.'

He drained his glass. His pale throat was prickled with stubble. She remembered the feel of shaven skin under her fingertips.

They finished the day's work in the garden together, then he showed her his preliminary drawings, on the dining-room table, for the Lisbon gallery garden.

He chewed his lip, then said, 'I'm not good with words. I mean, I can read and write and that, but not properly. That's what I need a secretary for.'

His father was a Sheffield copper, his mother a teacher, he said. He went to the local comprehensive, then to work cutting lawns at one of the big houses in the south. He sniffed. 'They treated you like shit, but you learned things.'

He had learned about gardens, started managing places, fixing things up. Now he designed them. He had started to make a good deal of money, was beginning to get commissions throughout Europe.

'But I've still got a Sheffield voice, haven't I?' He ran his fingers over the whorls in the wooden grain of the table. Then he looked at her, and grinned. In England they both knew what it was like to be from the wrong place.

'So,' he said later, after they had walked, leaning and breathless, back up to the house from the valley. 'What made you come here anyway?'

She scanned the hillsides, following the lines of the drystone walls. 'I want to learn about gardens,' she said.

He sniffed again, and smiled. 'I meant to England,' he said. 'But that's good enough.'

She had not seen Ellen or Sandra in the first years after the day they had all three driven in a taxi from Heathrow, Jocelyn cradling Sandra, half-asleep, in her arms. In the taxi Ellen had turned from looking at the grey streets and spoken to Jocelyn:

'Where will you stay?'

Jocelyn stared at her, felt the glass windows closing them in. 'What do you mean?'

Ellen's green eyes gazed back. The cab slowed, then stopped outside a house, and at the top of the stairs a door opened, and Jocelyn could see Thomas standing there in a dark blue shirt, waiting. Sandra sat up. Ellen put her hand on Sandra's arm and said then to Jocelyn, 'We don't want you. We don't want anything to do with you.'

Jocelyn sat in the cold taxi, numbed from the feet, not believing this cutting away.

But the cab doors were opening and then Ellen was running up the stairs into Thomas's outstretched arms, and the terrible birdcall of her crying sounded out into the street, and Sandra and Jocelyn were getting out of the cab.

Sandra's mittened hand gripped tight to Jocelyn's there on the pavement. Controlling her own voice, some-how, Jocelyn told her: she would write, and Sandra must write or telephone her if she needed anything, and she would come.

'*Do you understand?*' she asked, crouching, kissing Sandra's hand. But Sandra stood staring up the steps, shaking her head. And Jocelyn had peeled her little fingers away and got back into the taxi.

The last image she saw before the car turned the corner was her niece, six years old in a brown overcoat, standing alone on a cold pavement in a London fog.

She let the taxi drive on. She looked out into the drizzle that childhood memory had flashed back, of Ellen

walking away from her up the strange street to the crest
of the hill.

Once Jocelyn had walked past Ellen's Kensington house.
She waited at the corner for an hour to see if she could see
them going in or leaving. She begged Ellen by telephone
to see her. *I just want to know you are all right.* Ellen finally
agreed, and she entered the tea shop in Sloane Square
looking like a woman from a Harrods catalogue. Her hair
shone in a dark bob and her skin was clear and smooth.

They had been to Italy, she explained, on holidays.

'Thomas loves Florence. We go as often as possible.'
She said it like a declaration of something.

'How's Sandra?'

Ellen looked her in the eye. 'She's very well, thank you.
She's fine.' She relented then, taking a picture from her
handbag and passing it across the table. Sandra, her baby
face now slimmed and elongated like her mother's, stood
in a party dress in front of an oak mantelpiece. Smiling
like Ellen used to as a child, half-genuine, half only for
the photograph. Sandra's arms and legs were long and
slender. Jocelyn searched her face for clues, finding nothing
beyond the shining surface of the photographic paper.

'She looks tall,' was all she said.

'Yes,' said Ellen.

Jocelyn said nothing of her early London months, the nights curled in a narrow bed crying with homesickness; she did not speak about walking the perimeters of London's parks.

At the end they hugged, briefly, Jocelyn wanting to hold on a second longer but letting go at Ellen's first slight movement.

'It doesn't happen any more. In case you worry,' Ellen said.

Jocelyn nodded, said, 'Okay.'

Then only just stopped herself from asking if Ellen had heard anything of Martin.

Instead, she watched Ellen's elegant back walking away up the Kings Road, ashamed that she could not decipher the truth from her own sister's words. And ashamed, too, that now she could see that Ellen was well and Sandra, apparently, safe, and that she herself was left standing in a London street, the thing she feared most was that old weed of loneliness unfurling itself once again.

Soon after this day Jocelyn started work with Duncan, sometimes in the Cotswolds cottage, sometimes at his flat in Knightsbridge, then travelling through England and Europe. Then she began to have dinner with him too, in cheap candle-lit restaurants with jazz music playing in a bar nearby.

Here in the monastery's library she sets up her things. Drags the suitcase full of drawings and sketches, the dried leaves of plants, the photographs, articles, coloured paper swatches, and opens it on the large reading table. These wisps of her garden she has brought back, having carried them across Europe all these years.

She clears the shelves and sets out each folder, magazine, leaf. Crayons and calculators and rulers and strings and plumb lines. Covers the walls with the photographs and the drawings.

Last, she lifts out the book, *Botanica Australis*.

In her shifting of the old library books and her own boxes, she does not see the pastel drawing in a stack against the wall, of a Pittwater headland falling into a flat sea.

During the first days she moves meditatively through the buildings – the hallways, the bathrooms, the studies and offices and scullery and the flywired meat house with the smell of old mutton still hanging about it. In the dormitory she moves from bed to bed, trying to imagine the men who lay there at night. Did they keep one another awake? Did they sometimes climb secretly into each other's arms, from loneliness, from love?

Trying to imagine how these Irishmen could fathom a monastery at all, in a raw country like this one. Until she drove up the track that first time, she'd expected stone walls and gardens. Not this slight weatherboard collection of sheds and clapboard farmhouse expanded room by room, verandah by covered verandah. The cloister, even: a spindly thing of narrow wooden posts, a concrete path, a hot little square of dusty grass and a half-dead rosebush in place of Europe's colonnades and parterres.

The cloister quadrangle is flanked by four narrow buildings. The first, which faces out to the drive and beyond it the paddocks, the dam and the ridge in the distance, contains the library, scriptorium, the abbot's offices and sitting rooms. Along the rear of the building, all the flimsy flywire doors open to the cement path of the cloister. Opposite these doors across the cloister are the dormitories and bathrooms. On the left, nearest the abbey, is the infirmary building; on the right, the kitchen, laundry and refectory.

In a room next to the laundry she comes across a tall locked cabinet. Eventually finding its small key on the ring the estate agent gave her, she opens it and then takes a sudden step back. A gun. Surely they could not have meant to leave it. She stares, then takes down the rifle, holding it carefully away from her body. The cold metal and the smooth wood, its bony lines. She puts it back, locks the door carefully.

She walks the spaces, marking the beginnings of a

possible garden with her footsteps. On the bare dirt between the abbey and the infirmary, the physic garden. Beside it, across this wide sweep of thistle, could be a sacristan's cutting garden. Picking her way through the thistles, she reaches a waist-high wooden gate and a dark, swollen hedge of dying box – beyond the gate, behind the hedge, she knows, lies the cemetery. She does not enter there, keeps walking, at a distance from the dormitory, through the lame fruit trees of what must once have been an orchard.

Outside the kitchen and refectory are the remains of a basic vegetable garden. Further off, scattered around are the chook yards, a bore-water pump, a woodshed.

As she walks her eye falls on contours, spaces, verticals and horizontals. In her head a path forms, between the functional and the contemplative, meanderings and pauses offering places to rest, or transitions from one quiet way of being to another. At the front, from the porch, she stares across the dead lawn towards the paddocks and imagines shallow terraces; the murky dam becomes a pool, the merging of her garden into bush.

Each afternoon she walks a different part of the land.

She climbs the stony ridge, boots slipping. She grasps hold of whip-thin saplings to support her as she clambers through the mentholated air.

On this, the fifth day, approaching the ridge, she can see from the paddock a bald area among the trees. Scanning about, she looks for, eventually finds, a slight but distinct path trodden between the spotted gums and the lichened rocks, through the ragged bush. Soon she is walking through the pale trunks of the eucalypts, and the air vibrates with insects. Past a ledge of rock, and there –

The breath is sucked from her lungs.

Rusted iron fence, two feet by four. Under the lean of the trees the earth is scuffed with pale grasses and fallen bark. Jocelyn sifts flies away with one hand, standing on this crackling earth under a bleached sky, with the fingers of her other hand curled over the rails of a child's grave.

The fence is barely visible against the verticals of scrub and vine and sapling. She sinks to her knees on the rotting eucalypt leaves and the dry rags of bark, and holds the rusted bars of the fence with both her hands.

It is dusk when she makes her way back through the bush, climbing down the ridge. The change from bush to paddock has softened in this light, a tonal shift. Then her eye is caught by something moving, and she makes out a crooked line of kangaroos, there must be a dozen of them, soft grey forms in the falling dark, moving in their threaded ballet of slow loops across the flat.

———

Over that first summer with Duncan she had seen England's parks and gardens. It was 1967, but at Hampton Court, Sissinghurst, Kew, at others with forgettable names and famous designers, the centuries rolled back. Mannerist, romantic, classical, twentieth century. Capability Brown, Robinson, Jekyll. Duncan spoke of the epochs and monarchs of British garden design, the fashions leaping back and forth across the Channel, across Europe. The long-abandoned *giochi d'acqua*, the absurdly intricate, hydraulically operated stone-and-water puppet-shows that had sixteenth-century stone birds singing, dragons gyrating, stone hermits opening cave doors and gliding out to greet the garden visitor. The endless water chains, grottoes stuccoed with stalactites of shell and sparkling grit. The ramps, fountains, terraces, balustrades, overlooking panoramas of shifted, moulded, planted, shaped land. The centuries of erasure and reconstruction of thousands on thousands of acres, the construction, destruction, draining of lakes, diverting of rivers, the strewing of intricate parterres and knot gardens and mosaic and stone, and the madness of topiary in every form.

The Temple of Apollo loomed out of the sodden English air in a Wiltshire garden, its classical white stone a pale swatch against the green, the green. They had been travelling for weeks and despite her detailed note-taking she was tired of the classical allusions and the sump-tuousness of all this artifice. And on another lush terrace tumbling with hundred-year-old creepers, she felt guiltily homesick for something raw and dry. She had a surge of compassion for Australia's arid little postage stamps, the People's Parks of innumerable rural towns. Squat oblongs of fifty square feet between the railway track and the highway, half a dozen mangy pencil pines, hopeful patches of scuffed buffalo grass. Always one fat wooden seat, angled too far backwards for comfort, set into solid cement block legs, and positioned with almost a surveyor's precision in the centre of the park, lacking shade in the sweltering summer or any cornered relief from winter winds. The endless shreds and shaved corners of land through small towns in the rural districts. Hinkley Reserve. Herb Greedy Park. The Alice Ford Memorial Playground. All grandly named and cursively signposted in fading green on bleached tin, little shin-high drystone walls delineating these paltry half-green spaces, thor-oughfares, sidings, bus-shelters. The parks and gardens of country New South Wales.

In the evenings, alone in her hotel room, for the first time since she came to this country she began to draw images of plants from home.

Thirty

U P AT THE ridge she collects seeds, takes cuttings and runners from the scrub. In a month there are lines of small potted seedlings outside the woodshed. Rows of black pots with tiny green shoots emerging.

She has marked out, walking, where the new paths will be, from one space to the next, curving through the sacristan's garden and towards the abbey, meeting the straight lines between the grids of herb gardens, the vegetable plot, the physic garden, joining another arc out to the cemetery, a larger sweep down to the dam, through the paddock grasses to become a track up to the ridge. And from each one trail smaller paths, tributaries to smaller spaces, where a bench might be, a lemon-scented myrtle, a place for thinking. Winding back on themselves, parting and meeting, coming to rest at the one open corner of the cloister quadrangle.

Back in the library she writes, scribbles down what she has observed each day.

The potted seedlings grow taller, tougher, their stems matchstick-, then pencil-thick. These first months she spends weeding and turning soil, too, and watching the lie of the land.

And collecting stone, for the paths. For texture, for delineation, for colour. For wall and stair and paving. For drainage. For seating. For pond-lining and terracing, for enclosure and for spatial release. For transition, reflection. For stitching her imagination in basalt into the side of this wide yellow dish of a valley.

Thirty-One

SHE AND DUNCAN once spent two hours among the mummies at the British Museum. It was warm outside, and she had wanted to go to a park, to sit on grass in the sun. It had been so long since the sun shone with any warmth that she only wanted to be outside.

In Green Park the deckchairs had been full of people lying with their eyes closed, offering themselves to the sun. Some of the younger women pushed their blouses off their shoulders, showing the straps of their underwear, and had taken off their shoes and stockings. When she first saw English people baring their winter skin in public like this she had thought their desperation pathetic. Now, after four summers here, she wanted to join them, to strip off the layers of her clothes and just lie there on the grass, listening to the sounds of the city beyond the green acres of lawns, and waiting for summer.

But instead they had got off the tube at Holborn and climbed the shallow stone stairs to the Museum.

In the gloom of the Egyptian section the mummies lay, in various states of unwrap. The room was cold, and Jocelyn buttoned her cardigan to the neck. Duncan stared at the silver and turquoise jewellery next to the tiny coffin of a young woman. 'Look how small they must have been,' he murmured, holding up his own large hand, marvelling at the tiny Egyptian fingers.

Opposite, in a glass case, were the mummified bodies of animals. A cat sat neatly upright, its small triangular face a perfectly sewn linen replica, dark eyes and nose coloured with dye. The cylinder of its body was long and tightly wrapped, and some of the outer cloth had been removed to show the intricate, decorative pattern of the woven webbing beneath. Next to the cat were two falcons. On another shelf, less recognisable in their wrapped bulk, a small baboon and a baby crocodile.

As Duncan stood reading the tiny plaques stuffed full of words, Jocelyn wandered among the glass cases, among the preserving jars and all this painted decay.

Ellen's baby had been disposed of somewhere in Australia's Blue Mountains. Jocelyn found herself wondering whether that small body was wrapped before they threw it away. Alone, or with others? Buried or burnt?

She stared through the spotless glass panes at the lit

gold and the turquoise, the body's arms folded across the heart. It had been possible, then, somewhere, for death to give rise to art.

She plants two hundred eucalypt seedlings along the track entering the property from the road. Her back aches, it takes her three days to dig the holes alone.

She wheelbarrows the tiny plants from the truck, cannot believe they will survive the wallabies and kangaroos, or the frosts that still come sometimes despite the summer. She spends nights cutting hessian for the tree guards, days with a sledgehammer banging in the posts. At the end of a week, she stands at the top of the track and can see her work: an avenue of small sackcloth shrines.

Back at the Gloucestershire farm, while Duncan worked in the garden she sat at the typewriter watching him move back and forth beyond the window. When he dozed inside on the warm afternoons, Jocelyn sat on the wooden bench with one foot tucked beneath her like a child, a lone sandal abandoned on the warm stone of the terrace, and began weaving a halting mosaic with shells over the large table.

She had collected them from the gritty beaches in England's north on a trip with Duncan and, memory echoing, kept them by the back door in a bucket.

When Duncan was not there she picked the shells from the shallow sloping pile one by one, examining, turning over, running her fingertips across the cornets of them, then placing them gently, instinctively.

When he came out she would uncurl herself and stand, leaving the shells flotsammed over the table, and go inside. But Duncan liked to eat on the terrace, and without mentioning it, they began to dine carefully around the shells, putting plates and glasses in the remaining spaces on the tabletop.

By this time they were lovers. She had asked him once, gently, lying in bed, 'Why do you want to be with me?'

His face had coloured. He said nothing, and then: 'I told you, I'm not good with words.' Holding her hand and stroking it, looking at the ceiling. She could see the leaves of the plane tree at the window, and she pictured the hedgerows beyond the garden, the tiny birds darting. She could think of no reason to argue.

The table was almost covered after a fortnight, swirling colours and shapes rising up in ridges and dunes. After each day's work Jocelyn would sit, head bent with her black hair curving from under the pale blue headband, brow creased, chewing her lip, occasionally leaning back to gauge the shape. Then her hand would hover, picking out pieces of the wrong colour or a somehow unsatis- factory shape, and tossing them without looking back into the green bucket at her side.

Home from a London job, Duncan watched through the kitchen window at her complete unawareness of his presence. Once he had sat down next to her and picked up a shell himself, looking for a space to put it. But she had turned her head suddenly, and then he saw that this was not meant for him to share.

Now he took her a cup of tea, putting the cup down in a space on the table, not asking what she was doing, trying to force his confusion away. But all he saw was the smallness of this landscape of lifeless little shells. She lifted her head and smiled, took the tea cup and nested it in both hands at her chest, turned back to her mosaic. But she had seen his face – and finally she recog- nised it, his embarrassment. She slowly put down the tea cup and, still without looking at him, bent down and lifted the bucket. Extended her right arm into an arc, leaned forward and guided the shells across the table into the bucket. Duncan watched the shapes dissolve and the colours mix, and half wanted to cry out, 'Stop.' But he didn't, and he felt something like relief as he turned into the house away from the suddenly dank afternoon air.

Before this, before she had shovelled the little dry crea-tures away from his gaze, she had answered him one night, 'It's not *for* anything,' staring into the fire after dinner. 'It's for me.'

Each day she works on the path up the ridge to the grave, setting down stone for the steps. In this working rhythm she becomes all senses, all touch, the composted air so rich and dank sometimes she is nauseated. And the swinging rhythm of the shovel into soil and the pickaxe into stone, the shifting layers of the bush and its hisses and flammable air, all merge into an alchemical, moving mosaic.

Thirty-Two

I N NOTRE DAME she lit two candles. Then paused. 'For my parents,' she told Duncan. She felt his eyes on her, his head turned from where he had been standing, craning his neck to look up at the cathedral's ceiling.

As she lit the first taper she knew it was not for her parents. She did think of them then, buried together in the Blue Mountains ground, pine needles falling over the gravestone. The engraved name of her father beneath her mother's, each weathered shallow over the years.

In the cathedral a choir practised somewhere above them, the voices swelling the building into a vast construction of sound. She thought of her father singing in church in the mountains, whistling bird noises under his breath to amuse his children when the hymn mentioned birds singing to the Lord.

Here she could make out no words, not even French ones, only a layering of chimed sounds. Something about it here – the building, the hunchback story, the choir of human voices – made her want to cry.

She lit the second taper, the one for herself, and pushed it into the sand.

She gathered her coat around her and turned to leave Duncan to the architecture. But Duncan knew the candles were about something else, some other memory not meant for him. He touched her hand as she went to pass him. He leaned in towards her.

His eyes were clear there in the dark church, looking into hers. 'I'm not stupid, Jocelyn.' And he let go her hand.

Small, anxious dogs on vein-thin leashes trotted through the city. Sitting on one of the green metal chairs under the trees at the Luxembourg Gardens she watched a tall dark woman with a white terrier. All the women in Paris were tall, all the women's shoes unscuffed, all the dogs' hair washed and combed.

She thought of Alf, wondering if he was still alive, still where she'd left him in the vet's secretary's yard. She thought of him sleeping in the sun, and of Sandra lavishing her child's love on the bewildered old dog, who until her arrival was accustomed to no more attention than an idle nudge with a foot while Jocelyn worked on her proof-reading before the fire, or the tinny sound of his food bowl landing on the laundry floor.

The woman bent down and unleashed the terrier, then straightened and looked around to choose a seat for herself. The dog stopped too, polite, dainty, then suddenly scuffled its back feet twice in the dirt and bolted beyond the trees towards the pond. The woman folded her long body into a seat and took a book from her handbag.

Sandra used to try to teach tricks to Alf under the pine trees in the lower garden, with pocketfuls of biscuit or bread. Alf sat obedient but uninterested, staring only at the pocket on the front of her purple-chequered dress while she chattered away at him, trying to coax him to roll over, or lift his paw. Eventually, when he hadn't moved except to waver a little as he flopped to the ground and let his tongue loll pinkly out, Sandra would shout something at him and fling the biscuit on the ground, then stomp off, leaving him content and snuffling in the dirt. Once she washed him, cornering him between the laundry tub and the copper, and lathering him up with Lux flakes. After an initial struggle, his toenails skidding in circles over the wet cement floor, he had surrendered, shivering and shaking himself until Sandra was soaked through. Then they had both gone to sit in the sun on the front lawn, an air of exhausted truce between them. The house was filled with Alf's clean-sheets perfume for days afterward.

Duncan did not ask any more about the letters she wrote monthly, never getting a reply. The first time he asked, she said, 'They're to my niece.'

But he stood in front of her, so she met his eye and held up the page: *Dear Sandra*. 'I'm sorry,' Duncan had said. He waited then.

Slowly, placing the paper back on the desk in front of her, she said, 'I think you should know that this is not going to change.' She paused, swallowed. 'If you're waiting for something about me to be different, I don't think it will.'

He stood still there in the little hotel room with his hands in his pockets, watching the toe of his brown shoe, lifting and lowering it in tiny movements. After a moment he whispered, 'I'm going out.'

When he left the room she sat staring at her blue words on paper. Jocelyn was not sure that Sandra even received the letters, that Ellen was even still at the Kensington house. But the letters were never returned, and she kept writing.

Now she pulled the plant books from her suitcase and

read, and sketched from memory the pleached lime trees of the Tuileries Gardens.

Once she had written, *Dear Martin.* But her pen stopped, and she had gently pulled the page from the writing pad, folded it, and dropped it into a wastepaper basket. The sound of the paper hitting the tin like something ending.

Over this first year the bones of her garden begin to form, its spine and limbs and walls and rooms solidifying in the earth. She walks and drives the country around the monastery, collecting seed, visiting nurseries and plants-men and tree farms. Never talking much: a woman in a green truck, heaving the vehicle up and down bush tracks and highways. But mostly the truck only moves back and forth in tracks across her own land.

A September torrential rainstorm destroys a month's work in a day, washing all the topsoil from the terrace near the abbey, the earth slumped through the broken retaining wall like lava, and all the plants drowned. She goes about her rescue, picking them from the earth, repotting them, hospitalising them in a makeshift glasshouse while she repairs, remakes the stone wall.

Repetition is everywhere in this work. In the mistakes and their solutions, the moving towards some understanding, then its undoing, the trying again. In the seasons turning and fading and returning.

At night, her designs become studies in the perpendicular; and around the perimeter of the dam she constructs duckboards and plants sedges, the *Gymnoschoenus sphaerocephalus.*

Duncan had often talked, as he drove from one site to the next, about terracing, about the Hanging Gardens of Babylon. Diodorus, he said, wrote that the gardens were built high above the palace, in tiers like a theatre. The galleries were first covered over with beams of stone sixteen feet long and four feet wide. The roofs placed over the beams had a layer of reeds, huge quantities of them, in a kind of bitumen, and over that they put two courses of brick and cement, and then the third layer was a covering of soil deep enough for the roots of the largest trees.

Duncan liked to give these small lectures, these offerings of knowledge. She tried to picture the structures, the measurements. 'You'll have to draw it for me, I don't understand,' she said, more interested in the mythology than the mathematics. She thought of Nebuchadnezzar's grieving Persian wife, homesick for the meadows of her mountains, and his building instead for her these gardens in the air. The story of a man with room in his imagination for such a gift.

Once at Pittwater, after Martin had pinned a swatch of bubble weed to the verandah beam over the step, he had held her, laughing and wriggling under its drips, until she kissed him. That bubble weed stayed there for months, at first smelling rotten, then drying to a hard, blue-green tassel. At first they would kiss whenever one of them noticed it there. Later, as it shrank, they would notice it, but remarked upon it less and less. By the morning she left for the mountains, it had gone.

Her body aches all over with this work of imprinting herself on the land.

In the passing of the days and nights she occasionally steps inside the abbey again, to rest her head on the pew. In the coolness of that empty space she sometimes wonders, *Is a garden always a gift?*

Jocelyn takes the map of the property and lays a new layer of tracing paper over the previous one. Draws in pencil what she has done since the last version: the stands of eucalypts and the grass-trees, the grevilleas now hip-height around the abbey, coming into spindly flower. Over time, on sheet after sheet of paper like this, she maps in the paths, the new beds, the benches and the stones, follows the contours of the land with her pen, with pencils and watercolours. Eventually, the drawings plaster the walls. In the evenings she stays in here, drawing and reading. Sometimes she falls asleep in the old vinyl chair, the radiator's heat on her face waking her hours later.

She adds to her catalogues of plants. Grasses: lomandra, pennesetum, poa. Groundcovers: prostrate *Goodenia ovata*, brachyscome, *Viola hederacea*; shade trees: ficus, lillypilly, the West Australian willow myrtle. The particular pleasure of classification, of the Latin names, of their retrieval from memory, of their repetition. *Grevillea sericea, Grevillea mucronulata, Grevillea buxifolia.*

Is this prayer? These invocations that, spoken aloud, alone, summon some potential, some instinctive, butted-at meaning?

Thirty-Three

IN ARLES, CAFÉS everywhere claimed Van Gogh, his landscapes and sunflowers. The hotel foyer smelled strongly of cheese, and Jocelyn had to concentrate hard in order to disguise the fact that its stench turned her stomach. She laughed about the cheese with Duncan. '*Philistine*,' he hissed into her ear, his accent exaggerated, ridiculous, his arm light around her waist. Sometimes she felt herself loosening, could feel Duncan feeling it.

In the market herbs were heaped in great piles, vats of olives shone. She walked with his large hand covering hers. It was 1970, she was in France, a good man said he loved her. She heard music hissing from radios, songs about love, about *boys and girls*.

Australia was long ago. She was somebody else now.

Duncan told her the story of a virtuous young nun, Roseline, who was setting the table for her sisters' dinner when she fell into a religious ecstasy. The mother superior came and scolded Roseline for abandoning her work and threw up her hands in anger at her story. Then the mother turned to see a flock of angels hovering over the table, setting out the meal and preparing for the nuns' dinner . . . Marc Chagall had made a mosaic, *Le Repas des Anges*, the meal of the angels, in a tiny chapel in Haute-Provence. Duncan would take her to see it, the chapel and its garden. Another of his offerings of Europe.

In the centre of the chapel was a glass case in which lay the fully clothed body of a very small nun. Jocelyn took a breath and stared in at St Roseline.

Roseline's habit was white and new-looking. Her flesh, if that was what it could be called, blackened and paper-thin. The body was tiny, more the size of a ten-year-old than a woman, and the feet protruding from the long skirt were misshapen and flipper-like. A typewritten notice next to the case said that the body of St Roseline had been exhumed 200 years after her burial, and to the astonishment of all, was almost perfectly preserved – especially the eyes, which were as lifelike as the day she died.

Louis XIV had heard the crazed legend about a dead woman's eyes and sent his physician to ascertain the truth, to see whether these were indeed the real eyes of a cadaver. In his zeal the physician pierced the left eye with a stilette.

He was convinced, but the eye lost its brilliance from that moment.

The creature's eyelids were closed now. The teeth protruded. Duncan nudged her, 'Come and see the remaining eye.' At the far end of the chapel in a gold reliquary was a coin-sized faded ball, under glass.

The week before, in that square in Arles, Duncan had asked her to marry him. The square had begun to blur, and she'd closed her eyes, but saw only Martin's face. She had felt suddenly dead tired, wished for nothing but to lie down on the stones and sleep. And then she knew that if she did, Duncan would sit by her on the cobblestones until she woke. She had opened her eyes, and felt her mouth smile, and heard her voice. 'Yes.'

Now at Chagall's mosaic, with its dusty angels floating above a table set with flowers and fruit, Jocelyn could not concentrate, kept thinking of the stilette and the eyeball; of the taking apart of Roseline's body. Making a saint out of a girl who only fainted into sleep on flagstones.

In the cloister garden of an abandoned abbey, drinking tea from a thermos, Duncan had told her about the tradition of the cloister, the enclosed courtyard from Roman times. From where they sat the view was framed and dissected by the stone columns. In the centre was nothing but the bones of a collapsed box hedge, and the only view beyond was sky. The circular path for walking and prayer and contemplation. Around and around, Duncan had said, just the sky and the stone and your god.

Now, here, nothing in her garden is as it seems. She observes the spaces all through the day, and yet each day she finds she has been tricked. She has her designs, her drawings, wants to move through them like a reader through a book. But once outside, in among the weeds and the soil and the air, she's undone by the very earth; the angle of the rise is different from her measurements, or a marshy spot appears out of nowhere.

Or, as today, the soil is not soil, but three inches down turns to solid stone struck by her frail spade. She'd need a jackhammer at least to dig here. So the bed takes a different turn, following the contour of this plate of stone, now revealed by the spade to take up half the space she had allotted for the bed. Each afternoon the drawing from the day before is redrawn. The bulb of rock now needs something to balance it in the opposite corner. So she cuts a path, in an echo of its curve, plants it with the pennesetum grasses, their ball-gown skirts and long dusky flowers on bowed stalks yet another repeat of the arc.

Each time she sets out with a plan the space rejects it, pushing her elsewhere. And each time she must wait for the meaning to uncover itself. She begins to feel that working here is a kind of apprenticeship, some mastery only possible to learn by doing, allowing herself to be led by the place and some formless faith.

She looks down on the cloister every morning as she dresses. A divided square, half-yellow with morning sun, half-shadowed. At its centre one diseased and leggy rose, a sunken path of stone, a mat of tangled weeds. In the evenings she sits on a bench by the kitchen door, staring at this space without seeing, her head full of jobs for the next day ahead. To dig over the fourth bed in the physic garden out behind the infirmary. Collect the truckload of manure from the neighbouring property's cattle yards. In her bed at night she hears the desperate moans of the cows newly separated from their calves.

She stands, leaves the cloister for the kitchen to make some dinner. The vegetable garden has grown into a place of quick victories. At first it was constantly ransacked by the possums, wallabies, foxes, rabbits, birds, but the new fence, set two feet beneath the ground and taller than she is, now tends to keep most of them at bay.

She takes her plate of food back outside, this time to the front stairs, and sits to watch the sun fall behind the ridge, in that half-hour of yellow and pinking sky before dark. Across the old dried-out lawns she can see galahs nibbling the grass, and then the dark swatch of the dam,

banisters. Or spraying in delicate arcs over the absolute stillness of the deep rectangular pools. Until now she had never thought about the functions of water in this way, its life, the pulse it gave to stone and symmetry.

Afterwards they climbed from the gardens, up the winding staircase in the dark with the other tourists. The only light came from occasional vertical strip-holes in the plastered stone. Then Jocelyn was cold at the top of the parapet, looking away towards the snow on the mountains. Far below them the city spread whitely. She understood *oasis* now, the idea of green in a pale desert. Duncan was at the other side of the parapet in the shade, watching down through an ancient, intricately serrated Moorish arch at the tiny buildings of Granada. At the next frilled window space, a boy about eight years old leaned out over the stone of the window's sill. It came up to his waist, and he stretched out over it. His mother began to walk towards him, quiet but nervous, watching her son silhouetted against the white hill and the pale sky, framed in the window. The boy glanced back at her, saw her anxiety, and then purposely stood on his toes, leaning at the wall with his lips. The stone city dizzying so far below. He pushed himself still forward, angled, tilting, inching his hips further out over the parapet. Jocelyn's mouth dried. The boy's mother called out to him, her voice strained. Duncan moved closer, Jocelyn saw, close enough perhaps to make a clutch at a trouser leg, watching the boy's toes now only just touching the dusty ground. She imagined the child's view, all that swinging sky and white stone. The mother called out again, but now she seemed rooted to the ground, her black shoes on the pale stone, the pleats of her navy skirt shifting a little in a slow-motion breeze. Her face was white.

Then the boy suddenly thrust his hips and lurched himself forward – *Oh God*, Jocelyn heard her own voice.

The moment swayed, nauseating.

The boy flipped violently backwards, landing with a stumble on the stone floor.

He looked around, grinned at Duncan, then Jocelyn, and around at the other tourists who did not see him. It had all happened in the space of several slow seconds.

Jocelyn was enraged, wanted to grab him as he passed his mother, ignoring her.

The woman was silent now, and Jocelyn saw her eyes filling with tears in relief and shock as she moved to catch up with her son. She moved the strap of her black patent leather handbag further up her arm, smoothing the leather with her other hand, tenderly, as if to calm herself. She walked behind him, reproached the child in fierce, whispering Spanish. The boy stopped, waited a step for her to catch up to him.

And then he wheeled round, raised a hand and slapped his mother's face, hard. The noise of it made people turn their heads, but then, seeing nothing, they went back to their views and their talking. The boy, still smiling, walked across to stand looking over the edge with his father. Jocelyn and Duncan watched from their separate sides of the parapet. The mother was silent, motionless for a moment, and then she arranged her face into a benign expression.

Her cheek began to bloom as she walked towards the staircase. As she stepped neatly over the stone paving she stared straight ahead, adjusted her clothing, pulled at the waist of her blouse. Her cheek was red. The boy's father had not seen his wife. He and the son stood together near Jocelyn, looking out over the mountains, the father's arm about the boy's shoulders.

The mother held a hand flat against the wall as she took her first step down into the dark. She had done all of this before.

Jocelyn thought of Thomas. So young it begins, the hatred of women.

Afterwards, when they climbed back down the stairs, Jocelyn and Duncan sat on large wooden benches against the coloured tiles. People's voices echoed against the marble, bounced off the orange and green and blue and purple. The ancient stone bowl of a fountain stood at the end of the long pool in front of them. People's reflections fell across the slow green water of the pool.

The boy's violence, the slap, still hung in the silent air. The water lapped at the lip of the fountain's bowl, and Jocelyn thought about hardness and softness, about movement and stillness, how over a thousand years a trickle of water can cut through stone. She thought about Duncan, and whether she herself was stone.

Then she turned back to the new ponds and pools and the rippling water appearing now in the garden in her head.

The garden grows. Trees are taller than she is now, the blank spaces between the shrubs are shrinking, stems grow woody and begin to withstand the animals' attacks. The benches start to look as if they belong in their resting places among the plants, the ground is littered with shed flowers, seed pods.

She still dreams of catastrophe. On one windy night the tin sheets of the roofs lift and crack and bang, and in her dream the garden is covered in weeds and great sheets of land collapse. Salt leaches up through the earth overnight and this garden is the whole continent, dishevelled, poked at, stumbled over, pocked and burned. She walks her vast, destroyed garden, distraught, picking at weeds with her hands knowing it is useless, but through the calamity is some kind of other presence, saying *This is it, your place, this is how you live.*

In the dream the final garden is ancient, vine-covered, and she is walking through Eden, through Babylon, Gethsemane.

In the morning she goes back to work, unsettled.

A parrot on the lichen-mottled fence hops from one rail to the next, then into the grass, moving its head like a series of still photographs, an animation. The blotches on the fence are silvery, like land on earth in photographs from space.

They calm her. She is in Australia, she is in her home. Feels the shovel blade slice into earth. *This is it.* This is how you live.

At the beginning of her second year, the sacristan's garden has begun to flower: kangaroo paws, everlasting daisies, flannel flowers, Sturt peas, the bracelet honeymyrtle, tassel-flower, and grevillea, the bright green birdflower – *Crotalaria laburnifolia.* And down at the dam among the reeds there are swamp lilies, ivy-leaf violets, Murray lilies and vanilla plants. White and purple, green and yellow, red and black, colours with which to garland an altar or a memory.

And as the garden grows, more birds come. Rosellas, lorikeets, scrub wrens, honeyeaters, their squeaks and shirrups and squawks across the valley waking her in the mornings.

Thirty-Five

AFTER A BULLFIGHT in Seville she had walked in silence with Duncan, the image lodged in her head: the young matador driven, foetal, into the dusty earth by the animal's massive black force. The two pale soles of his slippers wrongways and upwards towards the crowds. His body left for some minutes, then later collected by attendants, and the doctor's smooth, unpanicked examination of him there in the dirt. And the shouting crowds, their sneers, the shame visible even in his unconscious slump.

What kind of history permitted this?

But Duncan had been passionate about the fight's beauty, its balletic power. He had offered it to her, and now she found it horrific. So he laughed. 'You think there's nothing brutal in Australia? Your whole country's built on savagery.'

They were sitting in a formal garden, before an intricate hedged maze, Duncan making notes for the Lisbon
project. She looked up. He had asked her again, last
night, about what it was she had left behind in Australia.
'It doesn't matter,' she'd murmured. 'I live with you now,
don't I?' And she had turned away from him in the dark.

Now Duncan was animated, eyes shining at her.
'What about the convicts, left in their holes to rot? And
the blacks? Has your lot murdered them all yet?'

She said sharply, 'What would you know of the
blacks?'

The blacks were not *killed*. Not now. But already
confused guilt was flowering in her. She remembered one
of the young Aboriginal women she'd seen mopping the
floor of Ellen's hospital ward, concentrating only ever
downwards at her bucket or her mop, on the small circle
of clean pushed before her on the brown linoleum.

Duncan was half-smiling, waiting, taking a cigarette
from a packet.

The girl at the hospital had ducked her head if a nurse
spoke to her, and never lifted her gaze from the floor, or
from her skinny hands around the mop-handle. She must
have been twelve. A twelve-year-old cleaning woman.

Duncan said, 'You said you lived with me now, didn't
you?' He lit his cigarette, and sucked in the smoke. Then
he stood up, exhaling smoke, and said, 'I wonder why

doesn't it ever feel like that?' And he walked away into the deep green maze, leaving her there with his tobacco smoke and his accusation. He didn't hear her calling, softly, 'I'm sorry.'

After La Sagrada Familia, the rest of Barcelona had been all geometry and lines.

It was warm, Duncan walked slowly beside her.

She said, 'It is a growth, not a church.' It seemed something outside history, dredged up, not possibly built.

Among the animal-sellers on Las Ramblas was a cageful of small striped hens, their fluff hazed and black. A handwritten sign skewed on the cage, AUSTRALIAN EMU CHICKS. A dozen of them in two cages, alongside cages of parrots, budgerigars, hawk chicks, owls, finches, a pair of quiet lovebirds, magpies. The bird-seller sat in a deckchair beside his cages, reading a newspaper. Smoke from his cigarette drifted up into the faces of the blinking birds. The dusty smell of their droppings mingled with the smells of the street: exhaust, coffee, smoke, frying fish. Weak sunlight washed the air. She stood in front of the emu cage for some time, but the seller knew she was not there to buy, and he ignored her. Duncan waited a little farther on, hands in his pockets. She wished he would stride on ahead without her.

They zig-zagged through Spain, circling and retracing their steps for particular meetings, particular gardens. They would go from here to Cordoba for the patios, then back to Seville to talk with a landscaper at a citrus grove, to study its balance of shade and ornament. From there they would travel across to Lisbon. She was sick of travelling, but since the argument about the bullfight she had been conciliatory, appreciative. They visited garden after garden, studied form and species, and she walked through their knot gardens and dipped her fingers in their fountains and did not let herself contemplate how many betrayals might lie inside her marriage to Duncan.

In the afternoon she lay on the bed and listened to the piano being played in the building across the lane. It must be a piano teacher's house, for the music went all day, starting at about eight in the morning. Stopping and starting, phrases beginning and repeating, over and over. She thought of Sandra, now thirteen, sitting at the piano in Kensington. She tried to sleep again.

In the evening before they started on their walk the piano music had stopped. She wrote to Sandra.

I am in Barcelona, in Spain. I got married a few months ago, in France, to a kind man called Duncan who I think you would like very much. He is showing me all sorts of gardens and other interesting places. Today I saw some emu chicks in a cage, and I thought of your book back in Australia – you might not remember it – about the joey and all the bush animals. I wonder if you ever remember Australia these days? I am sure you are doing well at school. I hope Mum is happy. Please tell her I think of her often. Soon I will be in Portugal. I think you might have stopped there in the ship on the way to Australia. You can write to me there if you like.

She put down the pen, listening to Duncan's quiet, steady breathing on the bed.

The piano started again. This time it was not a student but confident, easy playing. It was Debussy's *La Cathédrale Engloutie*, The Submerged Cathedral. Through the window came those slow notes, and into this Spanish room the Breton myth of the drowned city, the church bells and the monks chanting from beneath the sea, and in her mind they were Gaudi's cathedral spires, in a slow, centennial rising from the water in apparition.

She finished the letter and put it in an envelope, addressed it. Another message dropped into the sea to drift towards that other, unreachable world.

They walked through the city down to the water. She stared out to sea, looking for cathedral spires. They passed a tiny bar filled with men and their staccato shouting, and cigarette smoke, and light. Jocelyn would have liked to be sitting in there with them. The beer was cold in their glasses, they cursed. Their wives were at home. They did not have the voice of a good man telling them things in their ears.

It grew darker in the streets, and Jocelyn's feet hurt. Duncan said he would find them a bar, a café where they both could rest. They kept walking. They passed what Duncan thought to be the city's small zoo, behind a high brick wall. The evening moans of indistinguishable creatures fell away in their ears. Then they were walking past warehouses, a school, empty shop fronts, past an open door, with people standing in a room, listening or watching at something. Past a fence. She could smell the rotten-fish closeness of the sea.

Then the air exploded.

A bomb, she thought in that millionth of a second; her skin leapt, she jerked around for the shattering glass. And then in the next slow millionth there came a rhythm in the explosion and Duncan was grinning, shouting, *Flamenco!* over the noise, and pulling her by the arm.

They ran back to the doorway, stood across the road from it and watched into the rectangle of light, into the flamenco class. The noise of feet on floorboards shattered out along the street, up into the trees and the night. Through the doorway she saw a slowly wavering line of dark young women in trousers, men in black shirts and trousers, women in full parrot-coloured skirts, they were all young, they wore their black dancing shoes like weapons. They stared straight ahead, hands on hips, they did not know they were watched. Or they knew they were watched, they welcomed it. They had no music, only the clattering and clattering of their sharp and savage feet.

When they were in bed later it was the annihilation of the dance she remembered, the excoriation of the air. She wanted it; wanted the mess of her history to be cleaned away. And she began, in a small voice, telling Duncan of Martin, of Pittwater, of her dreamt garden. She told him everything, Ellen and Sandra and the baby, talking into the dark. Duncan only listened, she could see his eyes shine, he lay touching her skin. When she had finished, she lay quiet, feeling his fingers on her arm, waiting.

'It's finished,' Duncan whispered into her neck, and kissed her and it felt like something new.

They made love then, Duncan whispering and holding her. But once he was asleep, and the dark was quiet again, she knew that she had failed, failed.

And inside her head the only image was Pittwater's blue shifting sea and the twisted red limbs of the angophora gums.

Thirty-Six

U P AT THE ridge she plants young Gymea lilies, the *Doryanthes excelsa*. The green swords of their leaves fan to knee-height. It will be between four and ten years until the stems shoot up and the fleshy face opens up high above. She stares up at the sky, seeing a decade on and the outstretched fingers of its giant crimson heart.

She remembers the first time she walked up the hot Barcelona hill to the side entrance of the Parc Guell. An unfamiliar gravel path of hot dirt and spiky dry growth, and the intense blue sky. When she saw a eucalypt sapling she almost shrieked. Then she came upon the wobbling, lumpen stone pineapple columns. She stood beneath them, heart banging.

What is this place?

She had climbed the stairs and stared out, out, to sea. She sat down at the top, breathless, but not from exertion.

Something fizzled in her blood here, in this prehistoric place. Its sorcery. Bringing Australia to her and snatching it away within the pacing of a hundred yards, within an inhaled and exhaled breath. Sheer stone trees lurched out of the ground before her. She was in a melting painting, someone's hot dream.

When she came to the open, curling mosaic-seated 'square', she had been heartstruck, sightstruck. Spent the afternoon sitting there in the heat, her spine curved perfectly over the slumped bulb of the *trencadís* surface, tiled with broken pottery chips, as though it had been modelled for her. The colours stayed at the edges of her vision, kaleidoscopic and viral, during her walk back.

She remembers how breathlessly, back at the hotel room, she had spoken of it to Duncan. How he was silent, watching her blaze. He had nodded now and again, but impatiently, trying to rein himself in. Then said, suddenly vicious, 'It's a freak show, not a garden. Gaudi groupies are common here; I didn't expect you to be one.'

Jocelyn knew then that he had seen her drawings, and that he knew it was something from home she had seen there in that dry and arid park. She looked at him, then down at the tablecloth.

His hand came over hers, and he made her meet his eyes, and whispered, 'Sorry.' But one thing had germinated, and another had begun to die.

She had returned to Parc Guell as often as she could over the next days while Duncan met with the architects from Lisbon. And she walked the wide gravel paths under that Australian blue sky in Barcelona. She was unlatched and caught. She fingered the strange symbols, the tiny messages left by Gaudi and his workers in the ceramic chips and blobs: now crab, now fish, now woman's vulva, now maddened, arthritic scrawl. She cupped the stone lumps of palm tree trunk-skin in her hands, smelt the dirt of the path, tasted its dust in her mouth. She *felt* it, this urgency, recognising it from that Pittwater summer when she held Martin's book in her hands.

So now she spends the whole of two days in the monks' rubbish tip in a corner of one paddock, emerging with bits of coloured broken glass, pot chips, shards of plate. Finds other things too, surprisingly unburnt, shoved in boxes and buried. Family letters, men's jackets, photographs of young men with sweethearts, reading glasses, ruined boots, pornographic magazines, rusted hair clippers, hair oil, ginger beer bottles. Exhuming the buried relics of boys before they gave their lives to God.

Now as she walks in the bush here she remembers again and again Gaudi's secret hermetic *capelya*, the windowless, doorless stone chapel shrine in a corner of his Parc. Its crosses, its bulbous stone petals. She recalls his elephant obsession – the animal's trunk in the house's chimney-stalk, the great cement elephantine columned legs in the sewers' water caves, its creamy, ribbed palate on the ceiling of his home.

And Gaudi's plants. Acacias, palms, cedars, eucalyptus trees, cypresses, planes, elms, plum trees, and shrubs and rosemary, broom, thyme, aloes, artemisia, evonymus, daturas, hibiscus, laurels, rhododendrons, ivy, bougainvillea. Symbolic, medicinal, structural, ornamental. But he surely planted and drew and planned according to some instinct, some force beyond his own will.

As she surely does, now, among the quiet banksias and the scent of the stirred-up tea tree. Tending her own *capelya*. She lowers the eighth lily plant into the earth beside the red-rusted fence of the baby's grave and, kneeling, moves to the next station and begins burrowing a hole for the ninth.

Thirty-Seven

ONCE A MONTH she drives the truck down the rutted track to the gate, checking the eucalypt saplings on the way. For one three-month period without rain she came down here every day, a forty-four-gallon drum of bore water tied sloshing on the back. She weighed down one end of a hose in it, sucked the other till the minerally warmth hit her mouth, and moved from tree to tree, filling the well around each and watching the mud dry in seconds. A third of the trees had died or been stripped by wallabies, and half the remainder were strangled by weeds. But today, as she jolts her way down the track, the survivors' new growth above her, rust-coloured and tender, is almost transparent in the morning sun.

In the town she visits the bank, the post office, and the ugly little supermarket with its cabinet of meat and its few browning vegetables. Now, after several years, they are used to her visits and no longer does the shop woman stare in her husband's direction where he's unpacking cartons of breakfast cereal, willing him to turn and look. Now they exchange gruff shorthand about weather, road conditions. The woman still sometimes stares through the glass when Jocelyn leaves, watching after her, this stiff woman with her men's boots and her lank, home-cut hair.

On Jocelyn's drive home this day, through the cathedral columns of the bushland, a flash of red spins across the corner of her vision: a crimson rosella.

She follows the road; it winds, turns to dirt and corrugations. The parrot's flashing, shifting shape stays with her; a bright red hand against the grey-green curtain.

She rounds the machinery shed and there are chickens pecking about the grassy verge by the track.

Shit.

Into the chicken yard, and the feathers and bits of egg and bloody hen corpse lying scuffled in the dust.

Fox, again.

She hadn't checked for eggs this morning, had not noticed anything as she heaved the truck from the shed in the cold light.

Christ. Now she counts: four more hens are missing. She strides the chook-yard perimeter, checking each wire panel, finds the loosened hole near the henhouse where the fence wire dips.

Standing there in the dirt, she shouts out at the fox across the yards and the paddocks. Then a rage rises up, she kicks violently at the gate, a rusted hinge tears, the gate shunts and falls looser. Hens quietly flap outside the pen, scattering.

She crouches in the dirt, in the shit and the dust and the blood.

It is as if the fox has not just killed chickens but undone everything. Rendered it all pointless, with one under-fence glide ripped out the throat of the years, of the garden, of any reason for being here. And will always be out there, waiting its ruthless new chance.

No.

And suddenly she's at the gun cabinet, yanking open the door, taking down the rifle and grabbing a box of bullets, slipping them into the magazine. The cool weight of the gun in her arms as she marches the path through the plants.

Fox, is all she thinks, the rifle strap over her shoulder. Marching through the garden, grevillea feathers making tiny movements as she passes. Through the grass, down past the reeds of the dam, the gliding silent ducks. Across the paddocks, into the first scraps of bush. At the ridge and she thinks she sees it, a flash of rust tail. Fury blurs her, she hears obscenities from her own mouth. She heaves the gun to her shoulder, trying to stop her heartbeat, holding her breath, cheek to the metal, firing. The smell of the gun, the dark noise of the bolt sliding back and forth, flipping shells out onto the grass, the wild air, flurry of birds. She can't see the fox any more but she keeps firing and firing. She has never felt this white physical rage, the sky and the bush whirling, and she loads the magazine again and shoots at nothing, not feeling the pain in her shoulder until the ground is littered with bullet shells.

And then, in the shot air, the bush is alive with squawks and cracks, with thuds and fear and flight.

Now her shoulder is all pain, she drops the empty gun's impossible weight. It strikes the soft ground in slow motion. She steps away from it. And suddenly she wants to lie down here, fall asleep on that ground between the trees and the stones and cover herself with the leaves and dirt.

The next morning, headachy from tearful sleep, she puts down her cup and pulls on the work boots. Spends till lunchtime in the yellow grass, hammering and stapling the chicken wire taut again across the wooden frame.

Afterwards, in the garden she finds a little stone carved with a word. She crouches with it in her hand, thinks back to school Latin. *Colo.* Cultivate, she thinks. And worship.

After the rain in May that year she walks down to the flats late in the afternoon of the first sunny day. The viciousness has gone from the sun, the grasses beam green light. She walks the track, then stops to watch and listen. The air is all singing with insects caught in the sun, tiny buds of light filling the air. In the lower paddock she makes out first one familiar dark shape, then the next, and then the light is soft over the forms of a mob of kangaroos grazing; some standing stock still and staring in her direction, others bent, slow and busy. She realises small whirrs and almost inaudible squeals fill the air, and then she sees the grasses moving: hundreds of tiny birds, each wingspan less than hand-sized, flying at full pelt just above the grass tips, scoring that air in arcs and spirals, and all the flat surfaces of the green paddocks, rippled with the engravings of the skating birds, are suddenly alive as water.

Thirty-Eight

I T WAS IN Lisbon that Jocelyn had begun to think so often of the Gymea lily, the flame lily, that mammoth, prehistoric plant. In the bush at Pittwater she had come across, over and over, its giant green leaves fanning out from the earth, tall as she was. Now and again from the heart of one of those clumps shot the flower's wood-hard bamboo trunk, only just slender enough to encircle with her hand, rising above her ten, fifteen feet high, and then, shocking crimson against the grey bush, the flower's head. Enormous, frightening; part beautiful, part decay.

At Belem, in the cathedral by the sea, a life-sized Christ hung from his bloody nails. In the sculpture the flesh of the hands and the feet was torn ragged, the bones parted by bolts. The thorn crown sprayed his face bloody. Nearby there was a wedding, the bride tiny-waisted and white from head to foot. Jesus on his cross, through his blood and rags, an image of sexually charged agony.

She touched the concavity between the Christ's ribs. And, for one half-second, had the shocked recognition of Martin's body under her hand. But there at the dripping Christ she remembered too a bloodwood eucalypt she had seen at Pittwater, a stain of bloody sap from its trunk like a wound in a human arm. Every time she entered a Portuguese church in the years after that, she remembered her country and it was filled with red and bleeding plants.

Thirty-Nine

S HE CIRCLES THE dusty cloister, sweeping the concrete path, recalling every European cloister garden she has seen; the low box hedges, lawns, the intricate fleur-de-lis, the rose gardens and shrubberies, arranged in quadrangles beside four gravel paths all leading to the centre axis – tree, or fountain, or pool, or white stone Virgin or Christian cross.

In the middle of the garden were the Tree of Life and the Tree of Knowledge of Good and Evil. A river flowed from Eden; from there it was separated into four headwaters.

She sweeps, sweeps. The sun is savage overhead today, bearing down on the lifeless and stunted rose. She moves slowly, sweeping and thinking, sweeping and thinking. Not touching the cloister, yet.

Three years after first seeing Parc Guell, Jocelyn climbed the stairs and steps of Lisbon and found herself drinking gin in the afternoon. She sat by the window and wrote to Ellen, in the weeks curling up like a dangerous wave to the anniversary of that April day the baby died. She did not know what to say.

I am thinking of you now, when I climb these hills, and the sea is another tiled blue surface.

The window was dirty. From outside the apartment came the chipping of hammers on the paving stones, the men on their haunches in the street with their small tools, cutting the stones into pale neat blocks.

I am thinking of you then, and what it did to all of us. I hope Sandra is well and growing and happy. She did not ask after Thomas.

I am well. I am in Portugal now, in Lisbon. The fronts of the houses are tiled, and there are eucalyptus trees. I got married a few years ago.

Anyway, Ell, I send you my love and I hope you are as happy as you can be, at this time of the year.

She did not say, *Duncan has gone.*

He had finished the gallery garden. A modernist garden, with long narrow pools and low plantings, and vast open swathes of space. The gallery was angular and flat, a creature from space. It was 1974.

Soon after the garden was completed, one Lisbon

afternoon, they had found themselves wandering into a market, into a sea of secondhand furniture. Triangular lampshades on coiling metal stems, couches with springs sprawling to the gravel, scratched occasional tables, a telephone on a stand with a seat and a saucer-shaped ashtray set into the oak. Duncan sat on the seat of the phone table, lifted the receiver.

Jocelyn was picking over a table of opaque green vases and ivory-handled cutlery. She heard him say, 'Hello?' and she turned. He'd crossed one leg over the other like a woman, and had lit a cigarette. She stopped, smiling at him across the small gaggle of browsing Lisboetas. 'Ola,' he was saying, 'may I speak to Jocelyn.'

A woman looked up, blank-faced him for a second, turned back to her companion, they resumed examining the bottom of a bowl. Jocelyn waited, a laugh readying itself, but Duncan was not looking at her.

His face turned suddenly serious and he said into the receiver, clearly, in English, 'Your Martin is gone.' She went cold. He still did not lift his head.

Then he said, more quietly, 'I am wasting my life with you.'

Jocelyn could only stand, staring across the green glassware at him. Duncan did not look up. He took a long drag of his cigarette, then stubbed it out in the saucer, and gently placed the telephone receiver back into its stand. He stood up, brushed ash flecks from his trousers, and looked her in the eye for two long seconds before walking away down the bright corridors of other people's belongings.

She reread her letter to Ellen. A tram rattled in the street below.

She did not add, *I haven't heard from Martin.* Did not say, *I don't know why I still sometimes hope I might.*

A month later, two envelopes had been slipped under the door of the apartment on the same day. In one envelope were two pieces of paper: a divorce notice and a cheque for £100,000 from Duncan.

In the other was a letter, and a smaller envelope.

Dear Jocelyn, she read.

You must wonder why you never heard from me. Mum never gave me your letters – I don't know why she kept them, but I have just found them in the back of a cupboard. I am sixteen now. I have read them all this morning. I have always, always thought of you and missed you. In the cupboard there was also this letter. I am so sorry.

Love Sandra xxx

And there in her hand was the other little envelope, thin and flattened with age. Jocelyn caught her breath, and let the tears come down her face. It was postmarked in Victoria, nine years ago. She unfolded the paper, heard her own breaths cut through the rooms.

Her Martin had told her where he was, and sent her a prayer, from the Song of Songs.

Set me as a seal on your heart, for love is stronger than death.

The sweep down to the paddock is lined at last with melaleuca and banksia in a curled maze. On her way back from the baby's grave she treads the boardwalk through the silky grasses at the edge of the dam, to stand and watch the sheet of still water. The reeds have reached shoulder-height, replicating themselves in lime-green stands around the water.

Back in the refectory she trawls through all the monastery's cupboards for china: for the mismatched plates, the floral visitors' cups and the green cut-glass vases.

She gathers together everything but a few plates, some dishes for cooking and one cup. She piles the stacks up against a wall behind the old stable. Her ceramic pile builds. One afternoon she hurls a dish against the stone wall. And then the others, each smash cutting through the valley's air. The noise sets the crows whirling from the pine trees near the woodshed.

Forty

S HE WATCHES OVER the cloister as she undresses. She has been thinking of Gethsemane these last weeks, of choice. In a garden at night, a choice is made. To escape, or to continue. Reason, or faith.

She has not read anything but reference books for years, and she ransacks the library shelves for a Bible. Isn't the Christian Bible full of plants, and stories? Bushes bursting into flame, seeds falling on so many kinds of wrong ground, Eden with all its fruits and traps and beauties . . . Is it because she is so tired she cannot find a single prayer book left behind? In all the leathered volumes there is nothing for her. She begins to crave a story with which to rock herself to sleep.

In the days, to keep herself sane, she starts to list from her childhood's Sundays every plant she remembers coming from a vicar's mouth.

Olive, wheat, palm. Vines, grapes. The lushness of oases. Bulrushes, papyrus.

Like counting sheep, she begins recounting the stories in all their laughable excess, their rhythmic seesaws. Loaves and fishes. Cain and Abel. One, two. She walks, bends, kneels, digs. One, two. Forty days and forty nights. The good son, the prodigal. Water, wine. Adam and Eve in their garden of good and evil.

In the spring she manoeuvres a wheelbarrow full of garden tools through the sacristan's garden, the vegetable garden, along the path beside the abbey, the dormitory, and pushes through the narrow gap between the library and the infirmary into the cool of the cloister.

Taking the shovel, she moves to the centre and digs deep, beneath the rose. It comes away easily, roots rotted and crumbling. Gloved, she tosses it into a shaded corner of the path. She spends the day this way, digging with hoe and pickaxe and shovel, pulling weeds out by the roots, turning the soil again and again.

The next day she takes load after load from the rotted compost, spreads the stinking matter over the ground.

Another day of digging, another of spreading piles of manure through. Preparing the earth, but still her ideas are unformed.

In another week the paths are marked out with the stones she's gathered onto the flatbed of the truck from around the property. The large boulder stone for the centre she's rolled, lugged, kicked in increments over the months from the bottom of the ridge. Has given up, often, with grazed hands and once a strained back that left her bedridden for a week. But then each time she passes she has leant her body to it, given it another shove in the direction of the buildings. Managing, on the last day, by lying the wheelbarrow on its side and wedged against the stair for leverage, to heave the stone and the wheelbarrow upright, then pushed the barrow up a plank over the terrace stairs, and then through the sacristan's garden, through the gap in the buildings, then tipped it crashing onto the cloister walk.

Now, each day as she rises and goes to bed, she sees through her window the four black expectant squares. The wooden lines frame the paths leading to the boulder in the centre, pale and solid. The roughly hollowed cup of its upturned underside makes a fountain bowl.

But no plantings. Drawings, each night until she can no longer hold the pen, but nothing sets. Only rising and sinking, these stray images and edges of something she still cannot fully see. Half-formed beneath the water of her mind, like Debussy's magical church.

A month passes and still she has made no decision on the cloister. And then for a beautiful week it rains, turning the square to slush and sweeping the mud up onto the cloister paths in silty waves.

After the rain stops and the earth dries out she begins the first path, the panel of the paper design beside her in the dust. Sits on a cushion to work now, her legs aching sore from the days of kneeling. Picking out colours from the buckets of chips, pushing them gently into the cement as it dries. The drawings have taken shape over the months, the paths radiating from the centre, the fourth squeezing through the gap between library and infirmary, moving out into the cutting flower garden, then drifting, fading out in its sandy earth. She squats like the men cutting the paths in the Lisbon streets. She stands and moves back, stares as she once stared hard at Gaudi's tiled walls, at the Lisbon *azulejos*.

One morning she wakes with a crimson rosella in her head. She takes a piece of paper and writes an order for one hundred plants of *Telopea speciosissima*, the red waratah. She is fearful now, sometimes, of what she may be doing here, of what instinct guides her. Of how it can be possible for reason to transmute into faith. And she thinks of it all the time now, of a doctor sending her a prayer, and of whose paradise she is replicating here.

Gradually, over the months, she lays down her mosaic pictures, colouring the paths with the chips and the shards of all the monastery's crockery. When she has finished she stands, fetches a broom and a bucket of water. Sloshes, and sweeps.

The four mosaic paths are painted with memory: of the cliffs of the Blue Mountains; the frilled beaches and dark headlands of Pittwater; the lake garden with its dead silver trees; and the monastery's young avenue of euca-lypts in raging red flower.

And in the blunt, cupped surface of the stone, now filled with water, is the Gymea lily's beautiful, decayed face. In the centre of that face, two swimming figures.

Forty-One

THEN AT LAST, her path complete, one afternoon she pushes open the stiff wooden gate to the cemetery.

She still visits the baby's grave up on the ridge most days, climbing the stone stairs she has made up the sharp incline, picking dead fronds out of the way as she goes. The avenue of Gymea lilies either side of the path and around the grave is still alive, their green shoots toughened now into broad leaves, shoulder-height. And the rust on the fence is darkening and corroding. In a few years the fence will fall away completely, and the rods of the lily trunks will take its place.

She thinks of Martin as dead. Except that now she stops a moment after kicking open the gate. She has not wanted to come into this room of plants and wooden crosses, in case this last belief proves true.

The grass is thigh-high despite the shade of the Port Jackson fig, its trunk as broad as a piano, its muscular limbs spread low and wide.

Jocelyn searches the place, then sees the faded crosses, each only just taller than the grass. She counts – twelve men buried here, in three simple rows. The thick crosses are lichened over with years; there are no headstones.

She walks to the first cross she can see nudging through the grass, drops to her knees and pulls the weed away to read the name carved into the wood.

Ignatius, Michael Brenton, 1890–1954. A man planted in the earth.

She moves to the next, *Thomas, Paul Sheridan.* Only names and dates, no poetry or prayers. The next cross and the next, a boy of seventeen, a man of eighty, of forty-two, sixty, sixty, fifty-one. She stands and kneels at the grave of each life left here in this abandoned ground.

Only after the eleventh, *Paul, Sean Michael Dobbin,* does she realise she has been barely breathing. She moves to the last cross, puts both her shaking hands to it, smoothing the grasses away, hair from a brow.

Matthew, Timothy Ford.

She finds herself gulping air. She stands and walks back to the gate, cannot understand why she is crying suddenly. And then it comes thundering in, her shame at believing he has ever been here, that he has left something here for her, this always stupid faith, this folly.

This total absence is worse than death.

Forty-Two

THE WARATAHS ARRIVE. So she carries them, one by one, awkwardly in their heavy earth against her body, into the cloister. Each time she must let the plant drop, the weight of its roots and the earth around them too great for her to lower gently. A hundred times through the afternoon she takes a breath, hauls a plant in its wet, hessian-wrapped earth ball to the edge of the truck tray, and lifts it up to her shoulder like a heavy and sleeping child, carries it the three minutes up the track. It's hot, the sun bears down, the air crackling. The mosaic paths are bright beneath her feet.

At nightfall the plants stand crookedly where she has let each one fall from her arms, leaning, resting, waiting for planting. Pain runs in rods down her arms and her thighs, spreads punishingly across her lower back. She opens her bedroom window and stares down on the four sectors full of wavering plants. The night is still warm, the sky clear and starry. In this light there is something human, and something reverent, about these tentative things. She undresses and falls into bed, praying, as the first watery shifts of a dream begin.

One late afternoon she hears a truck coming, from a long way off.

She's bucketing the waratahs in the cloister with her bath water. There has been no rain for months but the tanks, amazingly, have not yet run dry and the bore still works. She listens, hearing the truck's low grinding purr and boom, but when she reaches the verandah and stares down the track there's no vehicle.

Then she turns and sees that beyond the ridge the sky is a flat wall of dark purple, and the cloud is huge, roiling and bruise-coloured. The thunder booms again, and then a sheet of lightning flashes the earth white.

She wakes in the dark, smelling smoke.

She had sat out watching the electrical storm through the night, praying for rain, but none came. She fell into bed at one in the morning, the heat still crackling, the lightning parting and splitting her dreams.

Now she hurries into her clothes, the little carved stone a nub in her pocket. She runs down the stairs, out to the verandah.

Through the dawn gloom she can make out a thread of red light between the dark mass of the ridge and the lightening sky.

She stands there, trying to believe what she sees. For a second she contemplates returning to bed. She walks to the kitchen in slow motion, makes a cup of coffee, sniffing, inhaling the air all the time to decide if she has imagined the smell. Trying to pretend there is not that hot, terrible wind coming up the paddocks.

When she comes back outside the fire has reached the top of the ridge, bright, moving.

Oh, Jesus.

The smoke is already stronger. She drains her cup and walks briskly, then breaks into a run. First to the shed, the water pump, dragging it down to the half-empty dam, hauling the black hose back up to the garden, up the stairs, willing the water out onto the wooden verandah boards, seeing it jolt out, leaving it there to run.

In an hour large patches of the top of the ridge are red, and the smoke is thick now. Palm-sized burning flakes sail over her in the air.

She stands in the garden hosing the building, thinking of clapboard curling up like paper, straining her eyes to watch the ridge. Scanning about her, running now and again to stamp on a spark, a bright flake landing.

Please help me, does not know who she is asking.

At ten o'clock she is on the verandah with a wet shirt wrapped around her face, and the sky is dark and the fire tears up through the grasses, and then her dam is burning and sending flakes of ash to the dirty sky. The ridge still smoulders beyond, the fire spreading to the east. She has hosed all the gutters full, hosed the main building and the abbey until the water pressure drops badly. But still she can't stop watching, standing unmoving on the verandah. Her throat burning, and the grasses alight, sending their flames eight feet high and the smoke sweeping horizontally along the ground before the fire. And then the melaleuca catches and makes a flaming maze towards her, ripping and popping.

She runs, tripping, crying, thinking only *Help me*.

If it reaches the eucalypts the whole garden will go up, the house. She's closed all the windows, pressed towels under the doors. In the abbot's room she finds herself kneeling beneath a crucifix, crying, and then she can hear it, the roaring eucalyptus, and she bolts through the rooms – *concrete, cement*, is all she thinks – down the steps into the dark cement laundry, where she has turned on the taps until the water runs down the floor and out into the cloister. All she knows is adrenaline and her moving limbs. She slams the door, yanks a dripping blanket from the tub and kneels, sobbing, rolling herself in it. She lies on the concrete floor coughing, and crying and whispering, *Martin, God, help me.*

It seems hours later, when it is quiet and she gets up from the floor. The stench is terrible and it's dark as night. She listens and listens, there on the cold floor, but there's no sound.

It is noon, and when she opens the laundry door she can see only smoke.

She wraps the shirt around her face again. As far as she can tell the buildings are almost untouched. She walks around the house, to the front steps. A huge patch of the ridge is black and smoking, but she can no longer see any flames.

The path up to the grave is bald as a scar in the distance.

She does not want to look around her at the garden, but starts walking, a bucket of water in her hands. She walks the paths. Miraculously, inexplicably, the ground is burnt only in patches. She's so tired she can barely move. Her boots crunch over charcoal, smoke everywhere, the sky bloody in the distance. Some of the plants still stand, scorched ghosts of themselves. The trees remain, she thinks. Through the smoke she can see the eucalypt trunks, but their branches end in stubs. Other plants shift in the wind, dry and fine as brown paper. Perhaps they are only ash.

She walks, coughing, through the smoke drifts, the bucket slopping water and sending up clouds of hot steam. She should be elated. She is alive, the buildings survived.

But the garden is a skeleton. Everything not burnt to the ground is blackened, lifeless, scrappy. She walks around to the terrace and looks down towards the dam. All the reeds are burned to black stubs. The remaining slick of water is oily black and the boardwalk charred, half-destroyed, still smoking in places.

She walks back towards the buildings, holding the shirt over her mouth and nose, through the destroyed cutting garden, to the cloister which she knows is unharmed.

But when she rounds the corner, through her coughs and hacking she starts to sob. She treads her mosaic path, understanding fully now that it is finally time to leave. She sees her work clearly for the first time, the ash and the smoke revealing, suddenly, what it has always been: ghoulish, uneven, an amateur's garish imitation of something grand. Nothing has ever been less subtle, uglier.

She spends the rest of the day and night in bed. She lies in the sheets howling and it is not for Martin any more, it is for her own failure after failure, up to her knees in animal shit or searching the sky for rain, or scanning the paddocks for wallabies, or for birds, caterpillars, diseases. It is for all the useless, fucking *pointlessness*.

She gets up, eventually, in the middle of the night. Stumbles to the kitchen and opens a bottle of whisky, then walks the house with a glass of it, gulping and wiping her face with her sleeve, pushing out air from her lungs, trying to stop crying. Back in the bedroom she starts pulling clothes out, drags a suitcase from under the bed, draining the glass and filling it again and hurling things into the pile. She hauls the suitcase down the corridor and leaves it there. In the kitchen she opens the fridge door for food, and then lurches – she's suddenly starving – grabs at bread, meat, pickles, a banana. Then suddenly, *oh no*, the scrape of chair feet on wooden floor and she bolts, leans into the space between the dishes in the sink.

The taps dribble brown water as she vomits and vomits.

The dawn screams of a cockatoo wake her, still in her filthy clothes, on her bed. She has got here somehow. The

PART FOUR

martin & anthony
1984

Forty-Three

ANTHONY REMEMBERED THAT first, decades-ago day when Martin lay on a bed in the square of hard sunshine in the infirmary.

Now he watched out of the window to the driveway, the road, and beyond it, the ocean. He had an ache in his kidneys this morning. He pulled his cardigan more tightly around his slight waist.

Today they would have fish, if Martin caught a little bream from his rowboat moored off the jetty round the bay. Anthony liked a little plate-sized bream sometimes. Had come, over these last years by the sea, to enjoy a rest on the verandah and, if his stomach could take it, a little fillet of bream for dinner.

The sea had a yellow look today, but when he closed his eyes out here on the daybed he saw a field not of water but of pale farmland.

⁓

The decline during those last years began to happen without them noticing. The trickle of novices slowed, then stopped altogether. The country out there had become godless and they didn't know it, like soldiers hiding in jungles for years after a war is over.

Until there were only six of them left, sleeping in the big dormitory in their narrow beds. And then, too quickly, a desertion and a suicide. Pneumonia, another burial. The abbot, finally, having a stroke while fencing on a winter morning. Martin found him there nine hours later, unable to speak, his eyes watery with the effort of staying alive, just until he was found.

Anthony said the last rites over their friend's bed, Martin kneeling by with aching shoulders from carrying the dead man in like a child from the paddock.

Martin dug the grave himself, nailed together the white wooden cross to match the others. He had wondered about the monasteries of Europe, the fields of dead monks buried across the centuries and the land, while he knelt here alone beneath the highest sky.

Then it was only Martin and Anthony, the two of them, trudging through their days, their world shrinking until it was simply a weary path between the sheep yards and the abbey.

Anthony's earliest memory was the sound of a sheep coughing outside his bedroom window. It had got into the house garden and it woke him in his room with the tall pale walls and his little bed, blue for a boy. His mother shouting at it, clapping her hands. All these sounds and him, three years old, lying in a bed and blinking at the ceiling.

When you are old these little things, he was surprised to find, come flittering back to you. Little birds of memory, hovering, landing.

Then the command came from Ireland to sell the land and everything on it, the order would pay the rent on a house, Anthony could get the old-age pension.

Martin did not want to be still there when the local hordes came to see the inside of the monastery for themselves. Making a circus of it, children jumping on the beds. Women clasping vases to their chests, dogs running through the scraggly roses.

Martin asked to be near the sea. It was 1974, and they drove like any other travellers on a highway. Stopped at petrol stations, money for the first time in their pockets. At first they were foreigners, counting out the coins, feeling a mixture of stupidity and excess at this new weight in their hands.

Now Martin came walking up the road, plastic bag in hand. He moved to the gate. He did not look like the young man on the infirmary bed any more, though sometimes, in the sun, Anthony could still see the resemblance.

He came up the steps, a hand open. 'Nothing, I'm afraid.'

Banged the flywire door behind him. A minute later banged it open again, cups dangling from one hand, teapot held steady in the other. They sat at the table there on the porch, watching the waves.

The first time Martin had injected the morphine Anthony was horrified at the skill in his hands. Then he, this doctor, had finally told him his story. And in two or three days, Brother Martin had almost gone, and this country doctor was in his place.

Now they drove to the morning Mass in a church not their own. Anthony wasn't sure if Martin still even knelt at home for prayer. Now there was shopping, and fishing, and talking. Though they were both, from habit, still mostly silent.

The shock, on that leaving trip, of all the roadside colour and size. There had been billboards for Coca-Cola, covered in frolicking youths. Another billboard, for the Hawaii Motel in a dusty New South Wales town, its cut-out palm fronds spiked against the blue sky.

There were advertisements for radio stations, for

restaurants. For beer. Anthony sat beside Martin in the passenger seat of the new car that smelt of plastic and polish. In the boot were their two suitcases, and the back seat and other space was crammed with belongings from the abbey. Candlesticks, the holy statues. The taber-nacle in a cardboard box, seatbelted into place. A panel of stained glass tilted under the back window, lighting up the inside of the car, green and blue. Altar wine in bottles poked into available holes in the baggage, Anthony's boxes of decades-old lotions and mixing bowls that Martin had not the heart to tell him to abandon. A set of books from the library, the Psalter. The car weighed down with it all, and privately each man felt like a thief.

They stopped by the side of the road for sandwiches pulled from Anthony's bag. Chewing, they stared up at the billboard for Peter Stuyvesant cigarettes, women draped all over it like tinsel. At that moment, for the first time in many years, Martin had remembered the sea-weed mistletoe, the memory filigreed like those from childhood.

All things pass.

The drive took two days. On the second morning they ate their breakfast in the bright dining room of a Griffith motel. Anthony wore his habit. He was stared at. Martin was suddenly protective of the old man, and he turned and glared at the young woman goggle-eyed at Anthony's aproned lap.

And seeing Anthony there in the too-bright motel light, Martin saw him as the woman did, a frail and blinking pensioner, and he saw in a rush that Anthony was old.

Once they got to the new house Martin himself was exhausted. They ate dinner from plates on their knees in the living room, two chairs and a small table the only furniture.

They went to their beds, over which Martin had tucked, at least, their familiar but too-small sheets and blankets.

And on that first night of no sleep in a strange double bed, the sea sweeping outside, that Pittwater summer had come flying back and his need for Jocelyn came reeling, reeling in. And set in like the steady rain of a flood.

Now the old man watched Martin hang the washing, two legs walking beneath the plume of white bed sheet swelling out along the clothesline. The wind gathered beneath it, billowing it, sinking, swelling.

You wouldn't know, is what Martin had said to him this morning. Then apologised, but the slap still hung between them. Martin thought he knew nothing of women, said how could he?

Anthony lay back in the chair under the blanket. There were worse things, he thought, than this sun on the face. Despite his unwantedness, there were worse things.

The sun and the willow's shadow moved lightly over his closed eyes. Further off, the flat green sea slid back and forth on the sand.

He swallowed again, dozed.

When they first came here they would walk on the beach in their bare feet, Anthony still in his habit. They walked morning and evening when the tide was coming in. Once they stood among the swatches of green weed over the sand, left by the waves.

'Like old coats,' Martin had said, but Anthony knew him too well, and they were women's dresses draped there on the sand, green with the night and party lights.

They had stood together, watching the grey sea for mermaids.

After a few years they bought a television, and sat watching it after dinner, first shocked, then thrilled by its flickering and noise. One evening Martin called Anthony in from the kitchen. On the screen a bushfire tore through valleys and plains. 'It's Victoria,' Martin said. They each stared, not speaking, at the flames and the smoke rising up from the bush-covered hills and pale paddocks, listening to the reporter's voice over the helicopter's noise. The landscape was familiar. Martin quietly left the room.

Anthony's dozing was filled with the sounds of the schoolyard behind the house. The primary school children's lunchtime shouts and odd thumps. He had not heard a child's voice for fifty years – and now the sound was frightening. They made screeching car-tyre noises with their voices, they groaned, grunted. There were murderous screams, terrible thumps, layers of it, the squealed and scuffled sounds of the playground. The sound moved, too, sometimes behind him, sometimes seemingly in front.

But all he could see before him were the bricks of the waist-high verandah wall, the red concrete stairs, lawn, wire fence, a parked car or two, bitumen, straggled grass. Then the invisible dip and then, wide as heaven, the ocean.

He coughed, swallowed. He thought of the nurse from long ago.

A child's wail went up from the schoolyard, then a shout, shrieking and running feet.

She doubtless had grandchildren now.

He coughed, this time into his handkerchief, a large gob of phlegm.

The school bell rang, slowly, clumsily. He could hear each touch of the bell's tongue against its metal. It was a marvel how instantly the shouts and wails subsided, moving in a wave to the other end of the playground.

Her calves and her nurse's shoes, her quick stride around the ward.

Martin came out. He began to smoke not long after they came to the house. He stood on the doorstep watching out to sea.

We are all lonely, brother.

When Anthony was a boy he would swing on a gate down by the sheep yards. His father would watch him from the shed, hand over his eyes, then move back into the black square of dark. Anthony was eight, he liked the feel of his boot-heels over the first rung of the gate, the upper rung tucked into his armpits.

At dinner his father said, 'What are you doing, swinging on the gate like that?'

Anthony could not tell him. Stared at his plate, chewing on the fatty lump of meat.

His mother said, 'Leave him alone, there's no crime in swinging on a gate.'

He could not tell her either.

But his father watched him from the shed, the way his

youngest son first hunched forward on the closing of the gate, then turned and leaned out with an arm and leg, out over the gravel, touching the gate only with one foot and one hand. Then to the other side again.

Years later, when he told his parents he was leaving to find out how to live with God, his father looked at him again. His mother stood at the sink, wiping tears from her eyes. But his father coughed and said, 'I remember how you used to swing on that gate. You always were an odd one.'

And still he could not tell them about it, how he learned the gate's whines and high creaks, and learned with his moving body to make them into songs, so that when his father watched him from the black dark of the shed that was what Anthony was doing; making the gate sing out across the farm.

Forty-Four

THE PAIN IN Anthony's stomach grows worse. At first he tried to hide the fact that he could not eat. He would go to the bathroom and run both taps to hide the sound of his vomiting. He still pushes the food about the plate, but Martin counts the vegetable pieces as he throws them in the bin.

Martin remembers Mr Ho, back in those days when he had thought medicine was only about the living, when he thought there was nothing more for him to do.

And he remembers that day in the infirmary, when Anthony had whispered, *I am here*, and held his hands, and given him love for nothing.

In the quiet of his room Martin kneels, he prays.

Anthony had not ever gone back to the farm, not even when his father had died. He had sat with Ignatius and wept into his arms when the letter came, but he did not go back. Instead he made the monastery's years into his own farm. He learned to make the Psalms into prayers and, like his eight-year-old self, to make his prayers sing out across the paddocks.

He grows thinner, thinner.

In the end he looks at Martin from his daybed on the verandah, from underneath his blanket.

He says, 'I want to go back.'

They both know which part of the monastery is in his mind.

Forty-Five

MARTIN TURNS ANTHONY over in the bed, cleans the shit from between his skinny buttocks, tosses the toilet paper into a bucket. The smell is foul, shit and piss combined. And there is the increasingly sour smell of Anthony's skin, as his illness slowly fills the air around him. Martin empties the bucket and the piss from the catheter bag into the toilet, squirts disinfectant into the bucket, washes it out again.

Anthony's hand on his head as he kneels, exhausted, at the old man's bedside to whisper the Psalms. With the morphine, Anthony's body grows heavier and more difficult to wake.

It is four o'clock on a Wednesday afternoon in the bright sunlight when Martin opens the passenger door of the car. He has pushed back the seat as far as possible, pushed in pillows and blankets and cushions to make a bed comfortable for the sleeping. He returns to the house, then stands in the doorway facing the sea, Anthony's wasted body in his arms. Straining a little, he carries his friend to the car, lowers him into the cushiony bed.

Anthony holds Martin's arms tightly, stares out of his watery eyes, breathes.

Martin starts the car, letting it idle while he checks again the vials of morphine, the oxygen bottle on the floor. He will stop the car every four hours to readminister the morphine. He has taped the cannula more firmly over the old man's fish-thin skin, the thick rivulets of his veins. Then Martin eases the car from the driveway. It is hot, a seagull dips in the air, and the afternoon light falls over the ocean.

He turns onto the highway and drives west.

They travel through the dark streets of the town, its surfaces shining from an earlier rainstorm. They have been driving for twelve hours. Anthony's breathing is changing now, becoming less laboured. He sends a fog shadow up the glass of the window with each breath. He has slipped into unconsciousness.

Now Martin turns the steering wheel, brings the car onto the dirt road south. The moon is high and full, and the country rolls out around them, glistening.

The headlights stop on the white gateway, the old bus shelter.

So much time has passed. Martin recalls the bushfire report from years ago, but if it was here he can see no trace of it. Even so, the track looks somehow different from his memory. Martin checks Anthony's pillows, pulls the blanket up over him and pushes a cushion further in beneath to keep him stable, then opens his own door and steps out onto the gravel to open the gate. Its loop under his fingers, the gate's swing on its hinges is easier than he remembers.

Disoriented, he gets back into the car; he's exhausted but adrenaline starts its surge. He is beginning to feel more urgent. Though he knows Anthony won't feel much, he drives carefully, the wheels rising and falling over the ruts and corrugations in the track. He keeps his window wound down as they grind over this old short road. At the end of the track, at the crest of the rise, he stops the car. He glances over at Anthony once more, at his sunken, unconscious face.

When he gets out again the air is still, and scented with eucalyptus. He is standing, somehow, in an unremembered corridor of high flowering gums.

He moves to the other side of the car and opens the door, sliding his arms under Anthony's half-alive featherweight body, lifting him, his child's gangling limbs.

Martin stands, holding his brother, on this old but unfamiliar ground. He starts to walk.

Anthony's breathing against Martin's shoulder loses its rhythm. His own breath begins to match it.

What is this recreated place?

He carries his friend slowly along the moonlit eucalypt corridor, through a garden that was not here before. In the dark are the pale shapes of flowers, and a pathway glints before him.

A pathway?

He begins to recognise something as he carries Anthony down this mosaic trail . . . through the native herbs, the tiny orchids, the violets. At last through the cloister's tiled entrance.

And then.

He stares. He is beginning to cry now, in rhythm with the deep staccato breaths coming out of Anthony like the last of love, and he carries him, kissing the forehead cradled at his shoulder, along the coloured map of his own old paradise beneath his feet.

And then he feels through his arms, through Anthony's wet face opened up newborn to his, through the sound of his own crying – he feels the last breath, the soft weight of his brother's life rising up among the opened florets of a hundred globed red waratahs. Shifting, and waiting, in the dark and holy air.

N THE DIM rising light, when Martin has shovelled the last of the earth over Anthony's grave next to Ignatius in the cemetery, he lifts his head to see her in the corner with her hand on the gate, watching.

Under the whitening sky the cockatoos and the currawongs sweep high above them, two people standing in a graveyard, with their fingers feathering over and over one another in the new language of a prayer they have always known.

Notes

The title of this novel comes from Claude Debussy's *La Cathédrale Engloutie*, from *Préludes, Livre I*.

For logistical reasons I have had Marc Chagall create his mosaic a few years earlier than he did, transplanting it from 1975 to 1970.

I drew inspiration and factual material from many sources including the following books:

- David Bergamini and the Editors of LIFE, *LIFE Nature Library – The Land and Wild-Life of Australasia*, TIME Inc, 1965.
- Josep M. Carandell and Pere Vivas, *Park Guell – Gaudi's Utopia*, Triangle Postals, 1998.

- Michael Downey, *Trappist – Living in the Land of Desire*, Paulist Press, 1997.
- *Gordon Ford: The Natural Australian Garden* (especially Morag Fraser's prologue), Bloomings Books, 1999.
- Mick Hales, *Monastic Gardens*, Stewart, Tabori & Chang, 2000.
- Colin MacInnes and the Editors of TIME-LIFE BOOKS, *LIFE World Library – Australia and New Zealand*, TIME Inc, 1969.
- Kathleen Norris, *The Cloister Walk*, Lion Publishing, 1999.
- Filippo Pizzoni, *The Garden: A History in Landscape and Art*, translated by Judith Landry, Aurum Press, 1999.
- Michael Pollan, *Second Nature*, Bloomsbury, 1996.
- Coralie and Leslie Rees, *Australia: The Big Sky Country*, Ure Smith, 1971.
- Peter Timms ed., *The Nature of Gardens*, Allen & Unwin, 1999.

Acknowledgements

My great thanks to the following:

For time and peace, Varuna – The Writers' House and the Bundanon Trust, and the Dark and Boyd families for these generous and important gifts. For the tremendous help of a new work grant, thanks to the Australia Council.

For welcoming me to Tarrawarra Abbey and telling me about my father's time there, my heartfelt thanks to Father David Tomlins and the monks of Tarrawarra.

For their generous help with my research, great thanks to Dr Louise Harrison, Dr Kirsten Black, and the doctors on the National Divisions of General Practice email list with whom I briefly corresponded, especially Dr Greg Markey. Any errors of fact are mine.

For conversation, space in their houses, advice, books and other gifts towards the writing of this novel, special thanks to the Wright family, Peter Simpson, Jane Johnson and Brian Murphy, Andrew Harrison, Silas Clifford-Smith, Bill Johnson and Ali Manning, Helen Garner, Tegan Daylight, Caroline Baum, Inez Brewer and Maree and Mark Tredinnick. Thanks also to my colleagues Graham Smith, Janet Grist and Chris Brooker for their understanding, and to my beautiful family for their steadfast, unquestioning encouragement.

Peter Bishop, Juliana Ryan, Anna Funder, Fran Bryson, Jane Palfreyman, Jane Gleeson White, Sophie Ambrose, Rebecca Hazel, Eileen Naseby and especially Vicki Hastrich and my energetic editor Judith Lukin-Amundsen read and gave crucially insightful comments on the various drafts. I am enormously grateful too for Fran Bryson's guidance at the business end of things and for Jane Palfreyman's passion. Again, my deepest gratitude to Bec, Eileen and Vick for keeping this thing on the rails.

Lastly, all my love and thanks once again to Sean McElvogue.